VIA NEGATIVA
A PARABLE OF EXILE

by
Omar Sabbagh

Liquorice Fish Books

L/FB 302

Published by Liquorice Fish Books, an inprint of Cinnamon Press,
Meirion House,
Glan yr afon,
Tanygrisiau
Blaenau Ffestiniog,
Gwynedd, LL41 3SU
www.cinnamonpress.com/liquorice-fish-books/

All rights reserved by the authors. The right of each contributor to be identified as the author of their work has been asserted by them in accordance with the Copyright, Designs and Patent Act, 1988.
Copyright © 2016 Omar Sabbagh.

ISBN: 978-0-9931682-3-9

British Library Cataloguing in Publication Data. A CIP record for this book can be obtained from the British Library.

All rights reserved. No part of this publication may be reproduced, stored in a retrieval system, or transmitted in any form or by any means, electronic, mechanical, photocopying, recording or otherwise without the prior written permission of the publishers. This book may not be lent, hired out, resold or otherwise disposed of by way of trade in any form of binding or cover other than that in which it is published, without the prior consent of the publishers.

Cover illustration, book design, layout and editing by Adam Craig.

Printed in Poland.

Cinnamon Press is represented in the UK by Inpress Ltd www.inpressbooks.co.uk and in Wales by the Welsh Books Council www.cllc.org.uk

Acknowledgments

The author would like to thank the editors of POEM and Lighthouse, in whose pages a small amount of this work (or earlier versions of such) was published beforehand. The author would also like to thank his editor and publisher, Adam Craig, for his infinite patience with the prehistoric grasp of editorial paraphernalia with which said author remains, ensconced, a dunce; also for the infinite benefit of his excellent editorial eye over this work, from rough beginnings, to final, chiseled artefact.

*For Mo, Mo, Fady, Shady, Ely, Mazen, Marc
and especially Robbie
(the sometime crew at Ferdinand)*

*This is the most important lesson that a man
can learn — that all men are really alike;
that all creeds and opinions are nothing but
the mere result of chance and temperament;
that no party is on the whole better than another;
that no creed does more than shadow imperfectly forth some
one side of the truth.*

Joseph Henry Shorthouse, *John Inglesant*

Thursday

As the late end of spring widened her Cedar-green limbs across the gin-hued air of day, across the puma-coloured nights, Beirut, city of whores and city of dames, proffered her staple echolalia. Each corner of the city was the locus of large encounters: a peripatetic array of spangled contrasts: between, say, nubile adolescents enjoying the first pulse and fruits of a rhythmic hedonism typically Mediterranean and, at the other extreme, wizened geriatrics seated on makeshift bins, chewing tobacco or tugging gently on cigarettes, the veins of their deep oaken wrinkles — as though limned with hardy intent across slabs of ochre marble — naming the world as much forgiven as unforgiven.

Passing by one-such octogenarian, Yusuf was making his way down Abdul-Aziz Street, hub of the hub of the city; making his way as though negotiating a medieval gauntlet. The gently downward-sloping street was pocked with kebab-joints, restaurants more sedately thoroughbred, clothes shops, boutique and sundry, opticians, cafés, both traditional and grubby as well as new-fangled and sveltely saccharine. But this hydra-headed kaleidoscope of exchange and barter, of loud and brash or slyly seductive voices carrying and carried across the smoggy air was not what troubled Yusuf's agonizing amble. It was something else. Not the spitting colour of the busy street, not the Syrian refugees begging for alms, nor the odd lottery-ticket vendor hawking his wares, every so often shouting the Arabic word for 'Fortune.' It wasn't even the compulsively hooting horns, which made up the background-polyphonic of any Beirut street. That latter was so much the norm, that any real noise, noise in its most native sense — that of a metallic, clanging irritant — would have been the absence of the honking. No, it was something else. Not the odd smug haute-bourgeois parking his jet-like Mercedes in the middle of the road, a good ten minutes, while ordering a list of comestibles from the local Bar-bar, not the tittering teenaged girls who gabbled in gangs, pointing at anything as an excuse to titter and pass judgment. It wasn't taxi drivers parked at each junction, almost piling on top of each other to offer their services, often saying, pro forma, that they'd be glad to get you to your destination for the sheer pleasure of the service, for the proverbial blue of your eyes. It wasn't the snaking battery of scooters rushing here and there, now by pavement, now by road. It wasn't the absurdly made-up Madames, walking with Ethiopian or Philippine maids in tow. And it most definitely wasn't the very misnomer of the politics of the nation: Yusuf had stopped following that over five years earlier, finding the odd philosophical problem more agreeable fare. Nor was it the angina attack his mother had suffered during the night (he'd swiftly dispatched her to her GP, so that was in hand), or that his father, his utmost bastion, was, geometrically now, showing the wear-and-tear of his age. It was something else. It wasn't for instance that earlier that morning he'd woken to find a long pleading text message from a taxi driver who used to hang around Yusuf's regular pub. A few months earlier, Yusuf had given this fellow about a hundred and fifty dollars to help him with his rent, and only after the guy had threatened to kill himself, spuriously Yusuf knew, but he'd been able to afford it. That decision had jarred earlier that morning, because Yusuf now realized that he was viewed as a soft touch, and that meant he was going to be hounded. But it wasn't that: Yusuf duly ignored the text message, firm in his intention not to give in, even were he to have the extra funds, which he resolutely did not. It wasn't that a different, and far younger chap, a film-studies student in his last year at the Lebanese American University, had begged him to act in his short film. That in itself wasn't a problem: it was flattering, and though never having trained at it, Yusuf knew he'd the kind of self-awareness to make him, potentially at least, a truly brilliant mummer. However, he'd been cast as a crossdressing pervert and, having given his assent to any role the guy might want him to act, it was too late now, having been informed of his purported role, to pull out: it would leave the guy with a serious lacuna in his cast so close to the shooting, and, thus, hamper his ability to graduate as a consequence. However much he wasn't looking forward to the role, Yusuf didn't want to be cruel. And it wasn't that a cousin of his had recently been diagnosed with schizophrenia. Indeed, it wasn't even, given that happening, the fact that her highly traditionalist parents refused to openly countenance the fact, thus doubling the problems of a young woman Yusuf cared about, and doubling those problems at an age, late teens, when life, especially for a girl in Beirut, was already a problem, a daggering set of dubious hurdles and hoops. And it wasn't that he didn't have a girlfriend; nor that he'd not had a stable romantic or, more emphatically, sexual relationship in over three years. No, he was, relatively-speaking, resigned to that. In any case, used to solitude he was never lonely: his thoughts were his friends, comrades, loose or taut, prodigal or sedentary. It wasn't any of these things. If anything, it was all of these things and something else ...

*

That evening, Yusuf was to be found seated, paunch-propping the horseshoe-shaped oaken bar at his regular, *Hemingway's*; to be found, that is, periodically sipping a distinctly Polish vodka cashed in a short glass peopled by, as it happened, platinum knuckles of ice. Still short of nightfall-proper, the sky outside the wide fronting-window was creeping from gunmetal to lavender to first-craven-inch-of-purple. He was the only client in the place, and Robbie, his friend, head-barkeep, was saying, now into the second month of their friendship, that the plight of a Palestinian Christian in Beirut was a wicked kind of warped conundrum. In turn, Yusuf had mentioned Churchill's dictum about a riddle and a mystery and a third recondite thing, and Robbie, piqued by the quaintness of the Anglophone reference, had smiled humbly and said, 'Yes, like that, just like that.'

Robbie was by nature hard, taciturn, but with those rare few whom he called friends, true friends, he showed a more lightsome side of his character, to the point of humour and that least-Lebanese-like trait: the ability to mock and laugh at yourself. Your average Lebanese is split between two extremes, both of which eschew any possibility or integral sense of sincere self-deprecation. You'd either the majority: rut-poor, religionists in the main, who'd interpret it as nonsense, wildly illogical, who would say: before God, yes, sure, of a necessity, but with your fellow Beiruti? Or you'd the upper-class: smart or sophisticated enough to understand it, but who none the less saw it as a sign of weakness and insecurity. To boast like you were sole possessor of the sky, or to flagellate yourself before the unfathomed sky-Denizen were the Scylla and Charybdis: but anything smoothly intermediate, well, it just wouldn't do, on the whole anyway. For all the wild and flailing anarchy of the city, it had its own rum, autarkic samizdat of order: the way things just must be, the nodal points in a Real of hunger and strife, or a feign-world of riches and high hypocrisy; you'd the dilemma here: to accept mud or to accept plastic.

'My life would have been easier,' Robbie continued, 'had I been born in one of the camps, you see. There, life is simplified. Without a single open prospect you grow into a freedom fighter, what they call a 'terrorist' in the west, in the way a leaf sprouts from a branch. It's a given.'

Quickly, he tugged downwards on his slim-fitting pristine-white shirt, a curt, nervous rite he often enacted.

And yet, what he'd said made immediate sense, because Yusuf knew that every licit text needed a context: if you'd only one possible line of development, however cramped, you lived, if not a happy life, a life un-harrowed by worry. Robbie had been born between worlds, so that every day of his adult life he'd needed to negotiate benighted hurdles if he was to win anything of worth. He was a victim, then, of the whale-large counterfactual.

Smoothing the side of his dark crew-cut head, he frowned angrily, then looked back up at Yusuf with a slightly-forced smile.

Briefly now, he excused himself to answer a phone-call.

'They always call at this time of day, postponing, postponing... Vintage Beirut!' He disappeared.

Still upon the backend of what Robbie had just said, Yusuf's mind wended back momentarily, a hollow distance of a couple of years. As he pondered, he continued to nurse his bison-vodka: toking on it unconsciously, an automatism, a steady helpmeet to this mood of wistfulness and slippage and recollection ...

'Smulla! Look at you, look at your generation! You have so many opportunities! And all this technology! When we were young, you had only three or four options: engineer, doctor, lawyer, or, homemaker. But you young people have a million, a trillion options: you are so lucky ...'

He was sitting in the living room of their family flat in the south of Spain. It was just after lunch, and he was about to enter into a chinwag with his mother and two of her friends. So Yusuf replied, without knowing what he was going to say until he said it.

'Yes, Auntie, but I guarantee you: your generation was and is a happier generation.' His calm and low voice was just as resolutely convincing as what he said. And then, perking up, now on a lucid train of thought, he'd mentioned a short piece by that Argentinean poet and literary magician Borges, titled 'Everything and Nothing'. It comprised of a two-paged monologue by a great thespian. In this short but potent skit, said persona listed all the great roles he'd played in London, Paris and so on: but at the end of this profane litany, the dying fall of the speech announced that despite this most distinguished career populated by such glamorous lead-roles, the one role he'd never played was 'himself.' It was a metaphor, Yusuf now said, roused, for how without delimitation, the human animal was rendered soulless, a victim of his world, not master of it.

It was his job, as a literature teacher, on the cusp of his first academic position at the AUB, to be replete with such signal exempla. His mother, at first slightly wary of his interjection, thinking he was going to gabble on some overly esoteric topic, relaxed when she saw he was being lucid and simple. Interesting, in fact.

Yusuf pictured his mother as she was then, tanned a honey-cream, and draped all over in loosely-fitting white linen: holiday garb. Her sea-green eyes were flagrant against the sunned and syrupy skin, and the ladles of bright light, which made that living room resplendent. She was, it occurred to him, both mythoi: that of the 'quest', but that of the 'foundation' as well ...

'And you know: this will surprise you, I'm sure,' Robbie now said, returning through the swivel-door from the kitchen, where the phone was: 'I actually didn't know I was Palestinian until I was fifteen!'

Yusuf had lost his concentration. So Robbie said,

'Hello! Are you hearing me?'

'Sorry, I was just thinking of my mother.'

'So am I! You must listen ...'

It was the year 2000 and Lebanon, however much reconstructed, remained a nation of shadows, ghosts, spectres. Like most teenagers Robbie had felt vulnerable: all he'd wanted was to fit in. At least seventy-five percent of the students at his school were Lebanese Christians and constituents or supporters of the 'Lebanese Forces' party — infamous from that wound in time, which was the Lebanese Civil War.

One day his school-buddies told him there was a rally in support of the party being staged at the Lebanese University.

'If you wanted teenage kudos,' Robbie explained, 'if

you wanted to be thought a man's man, a tough guy, even a sexy guy — in that environment you simply had to go along with the flow and support the party.'

(Again, now, the same taut rite, tugging downwards on his neat-fitting clean white shirt …)

Besides, Robbie thrilled to the thumping music, which blasted out at such gatherings; it was rousing to the avid neophyte, a vibrant call to arms, steep, dichotomous, Quixotic. 'In your footsteps we will follow,' rang the title, the stirring chorus of the most compelling chant.

And so: a thundering in hale unison, speeches in support of their still-imprisoned leader, coloured banners unfurled and unfurling like proper names upon the wind: the staple fare of politicking in Lebanon.

'Politics here remains feudal, a thing of patrons and bullies,' Robbie continued. 'One supports a well-known face on a poster.'

And that, Yusuf already knew too well: be it a fighting grimace or a winning smile. There was no incumbent notion of a reasoned discourse, of a plot, of an agenda or manifesto, however flimsy and false these might be in other, more civil, countries …

From morning till early afternoon, Robbie found himself cosseted within, and propped by, a sense of belonging.

'It was only when I went home that this, my small story, becomes something worth telling, my friend.'

His parental home was on the third floor of a building in Bourj Hammoud, a province next to Dawra, in East Beirut, close to Achrafieh.

'This part of Beirut, you should understand, was and is populated by a mélange: Armenians (all Christian), Sunnis, Shiites, and Syrians …'

Later on the day in question Robbie descended and walked across the street to buy some groceries for the house. On the first floor of the building opposite — and part of the gauntlet he needed to negotiate to get to the store — lived his paternal grandfather. The latter had spotted Robbie from his window and called him over for a word. At that morning's rally there were a plethora of news-crews filming and commenting and Robbie was captured centre-stage by one of these film crews, in flagrante as it were with 'Al-Ouaat' (Lebanese Forces.)

Robbie impersonated his younger self confronted by that patriarch — such theatrical lightness of touch being a tall compliment to Yusuf, which Yusuf acknowledged mentally. For his friend needed a stern and resolute demeanour with most, and in most situations, in the unjust carousel of his far leaner life.

'What were you doing earlier today?' his grandfather had asked. Robbie's voice took on a gravelly depth betokening the wiseacre.

He replied.

'I know, you jackass, I saw you on TV: what the hell were you doing there?'

'I was with my friends jiddo.'

'Don't you know who they are? Don't you know what they did to us? Don't you know you're Palestinian?'

'Palestinian?' Robbie had mused. 'No I'm not —' a pause — 'So what?'

He now chuckled in front of Yusuf, as if to dramatize his forgiving himself for the minor silliness of acting-out the roles. And then, switching sharply, more serious:

'My mother, you see, was and is Lebanese, and it seemed likely at that time, over a decade ago, that a change in the law was possible, that I would then be able to inherit Lebanese nationality from my mother's side. So neither of my parents had told me I was a Palestinian. Can you believe it?'

As it turned out, what seemed on the agenda never came to fruition. His parents' protective wishes were blown to smithereens. A seam opened in Robbie's life: to be a Palestinian and a Palestinian Christian in Beirut was still a kind of living martyrdom; at least until he fell in love, at seventeen.

'Till that moment, my dear friend Yusuf, my life was

a hard struggle, then a harder struggle on the shoulders of a larger struggle, and all with no ... what is the word in English? Return?'

'Reward,' Yusuf ventured. And, in truth, he recognized this heaving bane of an ill-starred name, 'Palestine.' And for which — however much he or his friend might question and pressure the dregs — they agreed: there was and is no euphemism ...

It was now seven o'clock and a few sporadic clients had just entered the bar, the bar shaped and hued so as to be readily suggestive of home-comforts, of an intimate hearthside. Robbie excused himself. The light outside was slowly vanishing into puma. Yusuf decided to leave, the better to avoid the lure-to-forgetting facilitated in so swan-like a manner by the booze. But at that moment, the owner of the place drove up on his chunky, horse-breasted motorbike and parked abruptly. Helmet off, his slightly-balding ginger hair dishevelled, he espied Yusuf making his way out and waved from outside for him to stay-put. There was a favour, it turned out, for which he wanted to ask. After a few pleasantries, seated together on one of the dark brown leather sofas, when he'd been brought a glass of Seven-up (he never drank at his own bar), Marc said:

'My daughter, Cynthia — I believe she takes a class with you? Yes?' His French-accented English was slightly comic.

'Cynthia? You mean Cynthia Khoury? Why yes, of course, she takes my poetry class. I'm sorry, I didn't know your surname. But yes, yes, now I can see the resemblance. She's a very gifted young woman, you should be proud, you know ...'

Marc's gladdened rictus became grave:

'Well, please keep this between us: I can trust you Yusuf, anyone who knows you for a day or more knows you're a man of honour, a trustworthy person ...'

'Fire away.'

'Well, my wife and I, we're ... we're separated now and there's much tension at home, regarding the divorce. I'm afraid Cynthia has missed a significant amount of classes, and not just yours. I …'

'Well, yes, now that you mention it, she has been absent quite a bit.' Yusuf then pre-empted, 'Ah, I see, you want me to be lenient regarding her attendance. Please don't worry yourself, I'll speak to her and arrange for some way of smoothing it out.'

Marc's face showed relief. Yusuf wondered if he knew his daughter was a lesbian. Not that it mattered. But twice or thrice he'd caught her blatantly ogling some of her peers, losing focus from some of the classwork. Yusuf was discreet. As a writer she was slightly handicapped, having in Yusuf's estimation more of a visual imaginary than a textual one. Her stories and poems were overly dense; though there was some deeply bevelled coherence, it wasn't in any way lucid or quite mastered by a sovereign artistic intentionality. To overwrite was the archetypal mistake of the novice. When he'd told her, she accepted the criticism as fair.

And yet, a truly appalling dancer, there was no doubt she followed in the erotic footsteps — if not with the same light-footed lyricism — of Sappho. He told nothing of this to Marc.

Yusuf's dinner and drinks that evening were on the house.

Friday

At three minutes past eleven the next morning, eased into beige slacks, sky-blue shirt and navy blazer, Yusuf began reciting the following passages to his writing class:

The First Crime

... It was a cold and howling late December night. In a high far corner of the house, Bassel was lying flat on his back, head on the lap of his mother. She was rubbing his temples, circling rhythmically, while staring down at him. All she did that hour was born of something in her which wasn't reducible to any description or paraphrase. Something deep and elemental looked out of her emerald eyes. If anything, it was more akin to flawless poetry. He was saying, in that high-pitched and hurried way that had become staple for him over the last few months, a product of his still-lingering mania, that he'd fooled the mind-doctor they, his parents, had taken him to see. He said that he'd gushed, veritably swelled, the wide spare room of the Achrafieh office with words. He knew (still bearing madness) the doctor would expect him to be uncooperative. But he had fooled him. He'd said all and sundry: come what may; as though the doctor were the final hurdle his psychosis (still the real, felt world to him) set before him; before that is, his evident Calvary and heroism won the heart of the girl. It was part of his madness to assume that 'she' was aware all the time of all his self-sacrifice. While this onrush coursed, his mother continued to gaze softly into his eyes, as if from beyond the world of time and space where his words were uttered. As though he might say anything, anything, but that she knew it all already, implicitly; and that all, in any case, was resolutely resumed in a mother's Care, a mother's unfathomed/unfathomable love.

And indeed, much like some late-coming Odysseus, Bassel remained a shuttlecock between that inkling of maddening siren-song and the very sea upon which he sailed, the very sea herself, tippling or hurl-gigantic ...

... For the first time he saw her was in the library. Perhaps it was the setting, then?

Because a library is like a hothouse for the libido; a warm abode for the mother of all intimation, Eros. No noise, talking, no food, drink — but sex is aplenty in the house of words. Not the act itself, but its real substance: the thought, the whole spectrum of that one sly intention, spiced by an all-pervading silence. There is a whole sexual sub-language, a continuous subterranean babble prolonged by the eyes of strangers. Over time one learns to read the language, to hear it: the look of desire as against the look of derision, the look of complicity as against that of enmity. But when he first set eyes on her he was a novice at these language-games. He'd no clue how to decipher anything below the rapture he'd felt burst upon him like a grenade. It was unintelligible, what the logical positivists he was reading at the time would have considered a nonsense. Clearly a proposition like, "She walks in beauty like the night," was non-verifiable. But that, immediately, with a raw, painful presence, was what he'd felt.

A more prosaic state of mind would have described her gait as lackadaisical, oozing an edgy indifference. She was wearing dark blue jeans, tight as a vice, and a fitting deep-red T-shirt. Not petite; not short enough for petite. Lithe. A little on the skinny side, perhaps, but striking. Striking, he thought, like a dragon, like some prehensile lizard.

He was a little woozy with the sight, rocked, quite seasick in fact. The precise lineaments of her image — the sleek body, the high drawn cheekbones, the dominant nose, the clownish smile, the blond hair bobbed up, bird-shaped — were heavy, ominous. For weeks he'd go to the library expectant of the thrill. Laying eyes on her for the first time in a day was like dying a few moments — where dying wasn't death, but a more intense kind of living. These are banalities of course, but to breathe it, to ache with it day and night, to ache, in fact, like a woman aches, was not only a new experience, but a spear of lightning shattering the glass of his insides. From October of that first year at college to the following summer, he became so much more fragile. How could the sight, the presence of a complete stranger erase so swiftly so much that was happy and strong and so firmly-set in him? He'd become a victim, without anyone doing anything directly. And every time he'd thought of approaching her, a needling hesitancy washed over him. She'd infected him with unquiet and inquietude. For the remainder of the year she took on giant, demonic proportions, bursting and bursting through the stone-hued walls of his mind ...

... A year on ... again, lying supine ...

Lying supine on the salmon-coloured sofa, his arms and hands laid across his rigid body, clasped there with the monumental aura of a stone warrior,

Bassel found himself weeping. At first, they were furtive tears, their load heavier and thicker for that. Then, like the proverbial dam, slow dribbling drops ran into combustive whitewaters. He was breached, so clotted with sadness, but not compromised — not yet at least.

So it was strange to notice the woman housekeeper, the wife-side of a couple who worked and slept at the Faris home, passing by the alcove-landing where he lay, hurrying past, her own eyes welling up in sympathy. It seemed strange, insofar as Bassel was able to process it, because he'd been so rude to her only a couple of days earlier. He had his pride, after all.

The Sri Lankan couple were savvy of course to the plosive tensions in that home. They knew on whose side justice lay. How many times had they been in the kitchen, say, the Mad-dam of the house coursing lyrical about this and that, and many a time, most often in fact, on the tart subject of her very son; her youngest child, the most brilliant, the most waylaid. And her rampant dialogues certainly weren't all of the tenor of sweetness and light, as, perhaps, they once had been. And how many times had they witnessed Bassel striding in, boiling with a boiling question on his stammering lips. Namely, to whom she'd been talking, and what of? For it niggled and it chomped. Especially as the Mad-dam would invent a name and a topic of conversation, which both Bassel and the help (for all their pidgin-English and pidgin-Arabic) knew to be brazen lies.

One day, in the midst of the usual imploding tempest, Bassel hurried into the narrow book-lined room that was his office, safe house — the arrayed books, his trusty legion, like counters and stepping-stones, holding the space of any erstwhile lovers, or indeed of any kind of intimacy. He was fuming with fumes redoubled now without a licit valve. It was, in truth, the equivalent of weeping — but, like a fetish, the anger was a stopgap for a lachrymose, more basic reality. On entering, dizzy and without any nameable intent, he found a sort of postcard, placed neatly on his desk, glaring up at him, incongruous. The picture was of Christ on the Cross, a crass variant of such. And the line inscribed on the back was from John's Gospel, something about life and light and darkness. It wasn't the idea or the theme that fused him deeper into a white fury. It was his pride, the atavism of it, looming and senseless as dodo or dinosaur. How dare she, he thought. How dare she enter my most sacred abode: and to offer solace. How dare she pity me! How dare she even know of my hip-wide lacerations, and the very crucible of my wounds! He verily flew out of the box-room with the kitsch postcard crumpled in his palm. Not finding the woman but finding her husband, he thrust it into his hands with an anger that stopped all words in their quick. He didn't explain but the man knew from Bassel's whole bearing that words would not suffice; wouldn't suffice for the mad and triggered vertigo of this in-wailing umbrage.

In any case, his wife was the catholic, not him. Thus, the flung riposte meant nothing, only that this young man, this boy, this boy who had, and who'd always had, everything, was disintegrating before his eyes ...

Yusuf read out these exemplary passages from his best student's work. Karim blushed when his name was mentioned, granting his permission; and after listening to the professor's admiring recital, literally all of the girls in the class looked Karim's way as though he'd a new and brilliant allure. He was something of a 'beautiful soul.'

The oldest student in Yusuf's writing class, Karim was a ripe twenty-two. At nineteen, it was known by faculty and coevals that he'd had a mental breakdown, a psychotic break, and had taken just over a year off his studies to recover. Yusuf had encouraged this talented wordsmith to put to bed this troubled past by writing it, making it his own.

At the beginning of the semester, Karim had told Yusuf, who was relatively new, of his staggered career at AUB, filled him in on what all the others already knew. He'd said he felt better telling and letting it be known, as this way, he knew where he stood, rather than being susceptible to paranoia, where he might suspect others, without knowing. This way, in other words, he knew what others knew.

'This way, at a pragmatic level,' Yusuf had said, 'you are taking control of your own story. Now, I want you to make that story into art!' Before being dazzled by the young man's keen artistry, he was already admiring what seemed like immense strength of character.

The first time Karim had smoked hashish was a year before the onset of his six-month psychosis. He'd been introduced to the stuff by one of his best friends, Said. They'd been clubbing somewhere in Achrafieh, and a girl Said knew offered them some good Moroccan fare. At home, they'd smoked it and it had been, on the face of things, if not a wonderful, at the least, a harmless experience.

The trouble was Karim's obsessive personality, which meant that once something piqued, he took it to an extreme. Over the next year he'd smoked all kinds of genetically modified stuff. But these kinds of illness were always over-determined: there were genetic and more contingent psychological factors which signified in his case. The girl mentioned in his writing was an Egyptian whom he'd first espied in the Jafet library in that first year. Now, nearly four years on, she'd graduated and returned to Cairo. But she continued to crop up, and signally so, in all of Karim's writings. She was like an idée fixe. Yusuf had an inkling of how this obsession worked, what it meant. But he wasn't sure. So he kept mum. His only rightful role was as a teacher, not a priest, psychologist, or parent.

'That all of you might be so brave,' Yusuf now said. 'A round of applause is in order, I believe?' The class applauded, whooped and yelped with camaraderie.

Camaraderie: it was something Yusuf had noticed since beginning to work in Beirut and at the AUB. Girls and guys at such a ripe age were quite capable of being respected equals, each to each. In the West, as in Yusuf's own student days, though there were exceptions, the majority of young men around the twenty-mark, saw girls either as prey, or as irrelevant. There was something so healthy and refreshing about Beirut, where they could be friends, and deeply so. Once, in fact, Yusuf had mentioned this impression and one of his students had answered that it was down to the remains of a certain, now quickly-vanishing, 'traditionalism.' Which was a good way of putting it. It wasn't after all exactly normal, in London say, to call the taxi-driver in whose beaten up Mercedes you'd just entered, 'uncle'. And upon disembarking, it wasn't the norm, again with a cabby in London, for him to utter a string of gorgeous pleasantries invoking the Deity to give you strength and sundry. But that was part of a paradox. They'd still God here, which meant, or should have meant in effect, the frail whiff of a Humanism. Except, for all the above, Beirut was the epitome of Capital's most fruitful gambit: a wild and viral form of atomizing atomism. For all the God-toting, there was no sense of Lebanese as just Lebanese, the idea that (under God) we might all be 'in it together.'

The same stellar student, Karim Faris, had put it quite elegantly as part of his response to the first exercise Yusuf had set this class — entries in a diary-format being the simplest task to set for openers. It was the first time Yusuf, as professor, had gladly noticed and singled out this young and burgeoning writerly soul. Opening his diary, Karim had written, flagrant with flair:

... Prime Minister Rafik Hariri died eight years ago today. Today's the anniversary of his murder down by

the sea, the mint-green sea. It happened just round the lip-like curve of a busy Beirut boulevard. A bomb, 1000 kg of TNT, had been planted to explode as he passed with his cortege and outriders: as developed and sturdy a system of security as any US President, I'm told.

It is Valentine's Day today as well — yes, that too. Serendipity has been busy, dizzy even, a rascal, a scallywag, as big a crook as any infamously crooked Lebanese. It's as if the kissing of the singular event and the yearly generic one were a message to us: namely, that the life of one is the life of all; that the human adventure, whether here or there, then or now, is one. That there is something, ghost or spectre we might wish for, make, or remember as Lebanese. *Though it be as slim as skin; or the idea of skin.*

Nothing's fair in either love or war ...

Yusuf, so impressed, had this passage almost by heart. It was the first time he'd realized that the great Prime Minister had been assassinated on Valentine's Day. The device was parsimonious. He'd even made a quip, at which the whole class had laughed, slightly nervously, to the effect that maybe whoever was responsible had done it on that day 'on purpose.' For Karim had made use of the 'Serendipity.'

And when one of the students had asked what 'Serendipity' meant, Latifa, by far the prettiest girl in the class and possibly the smartest, had said, 'It means the law of unintended consequences.'

'One way of putting it,' Yusuf said. And she blushed in deep plum.

There were times when Yusuf daydreamed with desire for some of his students. He knew that other members of the faculty had slept with students. He knew that some of the faculty, violently gay, had made use of 'rent-boys.' But beyond daydream Yusuf daren't go: he feared some sort of entanglement and scandal. Not so much that people, staff or students, might become aware of any illicit liaisons, but that the latter might be dangerous in a different way. A Lebanese woman was of the pith of Woman, but as regards pride, five times more explosive. Put concretely, Yusuf feared the high fury of their injured scorn. Imagine something went wrong in any incumbent relationship: the girl would have a wide array of opportunities, in that very unprofessional situation, to raise hell for him. And though not the most romantically-experienced, Yusuf had been in some situations in his twenties which only compounded this timidity: a timidity for which, in his more confident moods, bolstered by vodka, he often berated himself. He'd not had a romantic or sexual relationship in over four years. It niggled and it chomped: *this via negativa* …

At two o'clock, finished with classes, Yusuf had a three-hour nap in the departmental lounge. Having drinking plans that evening he decided not to return to Verdun. He'd sleep 'till the start of evening and thus, still in *Hamra*, make his way to *Hemingway's*.

*

One of Yusuf's few friends in the department was a fellow literature and writing teacher, an Afghani chap, Teymour. This guy had no such qualms. A frequent drinking-buddy, he'd regale Yusuf with wondrous tales of seduction, or near-seduction. Of average height, medium build, usually dressed in jeans and loose-fitting blue shirt, a man in his mid-fifties, married with kids (these latter back in Manchester or Liverpool or wherever), he was a storyteller, not only by profession but also in the manner of his friendship.

Friday night, then, and there they were, on cue, boon-companions at *Hemingway's* on one far side of *Hamra*. Not that they, both of them, abstained from the booze on weekdays, but rather that, as Teymour had once put it, it was necessary to drape this night in particular. He'd theorized once:

'Mate, it's like this: say there's a film, a good film, you've seen a hundred times. Yes? Then one day they put the film on the BBC — not the extortionate cinema, not the Sky or satellite malarkey, but straightforward BBC. It behoves you, don't you see, to watch it again: precisely because it's free. That's, in my philosophy, how drinking on a Friday or Saturday night relates to the other, just as worthy mind you, drinking nights.' He'd bellowed; Yusuf had tittered.

Robbie now placed their drinks on the table. Though never articulated, Yusuf always sensed that Robbie disliked Teymour. The latter now, lifting his glass of wine, said,

'You still haven't visited my apartment, old man. The fig-wine awaits you.' Having the kinds of financial exigencies Yusuf hadn't, Teymour would find truly canny ways of economizing in whatever country he landed. For instance, he'd bought sack-fulls of figs in order to make homemade wine. And this home-brewed fare was the staple for the teeming advents of his friendly hospitality.

'You know,' he said, 'the other night I'd this woman, a teacher at AUB — but I won't mention names for obvious reasons, old man — splayed on the carpet of my living room. We were messing around, you know. And then we got to just that point of no-return —' he grinned and his pupils widened — 'when suddenly, she switched off, became frigid as ice. What's wrong with these people? I mean I've students who get busier than that.'

'So have I,' Yusuf replied. 'So have I.'

'Yeah, but you don't even try. You make no efforts. You really should try and wet your beak, old man. Some of these girls are begging for it. Especially from their profs. You're mad, you know, not to take advantage. And you: a good-looking chap, if a bit chubby round the edges. It's the authority, the prestige that makes us so sexy. It's just as much a conquest for them as for us. Go on, mate, tell me you'll try. That gorgeous specimen, Latifa Jallad, I know for a fact that ...' He paused here, besotted by a quandary.

'Latifa, yes, go on ...?'

'Oh, I'm not sure: just something I overheard the other day after class. A friend of hers I assume. Your name was mentioned ...' Teymour had a mischievous grin.

'But what am I supposed to do with something like

that?'

'Listen, old man, it's your God-given duty to give it a go. Don't let the team down. And it's you who'll have to make the first move. I mean: that's obvious from the dynamic.'

'First move?' Yusuf gulped some vodka. 'Like what? Keep her after class and ask her for a drink? C'mon, you know if I did that it'd be spread across the whole campus, from Oval to Medical Gate before I reached my office. You're reckless, mad.'

'Maybe.' The idea wasn't insulting: flattering rather. 'But she's prime totty, mate. Gorgeous: tits, hips, ass. *Ooo ... I would!* And none of that stupid modesty business, none of that reverse-psychology crap. You tried that once: and it got you nowhere. And thank God for that! Taught you a lesson, I hope.'

Just under a year earlier, a woman of around the same age but gorgeously honey-made, had practically offered herself on a platter, and within five minutes of acquaintance. Though attracted, Yusuf had told her in the end that she 'intimidated' him — that than which there is no more fearsome anathema, awful shibboleth. When he'd told Teymour, the latter had almost struck Yusuf with his shoe — it was such god-damned stupid a thing to say: even *if* it were true. He'd refused to talk to Yusuf for over a week, by way of punishment. And then, on resuming their boon-companionship he'd forced Yusuf to make an oath, not upon the Bible or the Koran, but upon the one copy he had of Yusuf's first book of poetry. To never utter such an imbecilic statement to a woman again, be she ugly as a harpy. Yusuf had promised, not quite knowing whether his friend was in earnest or jest, or some combination of the two.

'On another note: it just occurred to me, after one of my classes earlier, that there is a strong possibility that Jane Austen was from Beirut.'

Teymour enticed the playful conceit. 'Yes. And Sheikh-spear.'

'I mean, that opening sentence "universally

acknowledged" about a loaded guy in search of a wife: that just is Beirut. Weddings and deaths, that's what this society revolves around.'

'Yes. Like famished carrion-birds, whether in felicitation or in condolence. OK. Go on.'

'And it occurred to me that there's a similar dynamic to sex here as there was in nineteenth century England. I mean it's not like people stopped having desire or sex: it's just that there grew up a kind of hypocritical Puritanical façade, which outlawed talk or recognition of such. Don't you think there's something similar afoot here?'

Teymour pondered, twisting his head at a diagonal towards the ceiling.

'In any case, it made for a good class.'

Robbie asked them for any last orders.

The two men declined. Robbie nodded sternly, in silence. Then Yusuf jumped into a taxi to Verdun, Teymour planning on a drunken ramble to the other side of *Ras Beirut*, where his apartment lay, upon the middle of a curving, downward sloping hill.

'I think I'll have a couple of swigs of the fig-wine, old man. Give the bedbugs a bit of a fright.' And he ambled off, swaying. Just as Yusuf's cab lost sight of him, he heard and saw Teymour begin to burst into some kind of Ghazal: bulbuls and wine and nude, lascivious women being central, signal …

During the six-minute cab-ride home, Yusuf was thinking how much Teymour resembled his recently deceased uncle. Seamlessly, swayed and tinted by the drink, he slipped into daydream again …

That brown monkish head with its grey moustache shaped like a stunted horseshoe wagging itself into animation; that mouth of black-yellow tobacco-stained lips with three front teeth missing chattering away; watching the life emerge in those big brown watery eyes, deeply inset above a Roman, pockmarked nose that exploded from his face like a second-hand shotgun. Yes, he, too, had ribald skill as a raconteur.

Yusuf could remember scenes with him towards the end of his life, near verbatim ...

'You know, Yusuf, the best place to pick up loose women?' he'd once asked suddenly, breaking the silence between them, his eyebrows stretched to the uppermost limit, as if attempting to query the heavens themselves. It was five or six years earlier, while Yusuf was still based in London. 'I'll tell you.

'Tell me, have you ever been to the top floor of Harvey Nicks?'

'No *khalo*, why?'

'Aaah ... well, habeebee, I'll tell you why. Because ... simply because ... all the saleswomen who work in the department store go there after work. And they're just waiting, just *begging* to be picked up.

'I remember this one time. I walked in one night and went up to Jimmy — he was the barman, a friend — I used to tip him the odd fifty pounds you know, so he would do a little of the donkey work for me, you know, the sniffing out ... Jimmy pointed to a little booth on one side of the bar where a young lady —' at these last two words his uncle's whole face creased up in a chivalrous, affectionate, sentimental, nostalgic smile — 'a young lady was sitting. She was dark you know, very dark, but sexy, sexy ... Oehh my Gaahhd, you should have seen her ... I was enchanted. Her legs were crossed, you know, but somehow that closing of the gate seems to enlarge the goal in imagination by a factor of a thousand —' and he quickly tried to gesture this factor, a retired economist, by counting along his fingers. 'By a factor of a thousand, in imagination though, in imagination, you know ... Oehh my Gaahhd,' he ejaculated, slapping his forehead with his right palm.

'I almost kissed Jimmy! Anyhow, to make a long story short, I went up to her and we talked. That's very important by the way, Yusuf — when you want to pick up a woman, you must, you must talk to her. Even professionals ...

'So things went well ... After an hour I had her eating out of my palm, and as far as I knew she wasn't a professional, not even a professional! I mean look how she was dressed —' and with his left arm outstretched, palm upwards, he described a semi-circle in the air in front of his nephew, as if to physically display the woman.

'Yes, she was an elegant woman, graceful, you know. So she agreed to come back to my apartment. Fine. Great, I thought. And then, just as we were leaving, you know what she said to me? Can you believe it, I mean can you imagine?'

Satisfied, he continued:

'She said it would cost me five thousand pounds. Five large! Who the hell did she think she was: the Whore of Babylon? So I said, "No way, bitch, no fucking way. What d'you take me for: a *jackass*?"'

Yusuf remembered having giggled at this; indeed, giggled now, again. There was something brilliant about the way is uncle could enunciate the word "jackass".

'Bitch. Anyway, I found out from Jimmy later, after I asked him what was what, that she'd managed to screw three hundred grand out of a Saudi prince a few months earlier. You know these Saudi *ass*holes. She thought she was only fit to go with men who had money to burn. I'm telling you, Yusuf, you'll see when you're a little older, some of these women, in my day, oooooo, they used to *mint* money. They *minted* it!'

He was a pedant and a clown, Yusuf now murmured aloud. The taxi-driver, veering-in to the pavement aside his building, said, '*Shoo?*'

'*Ma Shee. Kunt 'am Ihlam.*' It was his way to be dreamy. He thanked the driver, who in turn invoked the Deity to protect and strengthen Yusuf for a million days, in return for the price of a meagre drink.

Yusuf collapsed fully-clothed onto his bed and fell into snoring before his father could get up, rickety and old, from the den where he slummed, watching political thrillers hours on end, to reprimand his son, though in his early-thirties, for over-indulging the drink.

Saturday

Slumbering 'till noon-ish, Yusuf woke up, still heady with the thought of his passed uncle. Seated at his desk he decided not to make the same mistake twice. He'd still one maternal uncle living. Feeling word-pregnant and a little light-hearted after a sound sleep, he penned a quick skit and sent it to him.

Zhubrowka, I Love You

It starts like a tinker, tinkering, the ready tongue almost thinking, pressed, a quest, against the short cold glass. Specifically, I'll not abide a slice of lemon or lime: let the ice cubes render unto Caesar, larger than acorns, littler than conkers — those hardened artefacts, roseate-brown, at the heart of games played, mock-battles wrought, roughly in the chill or warmth — depending — of what was supposed to be my latency period. Small girls, indeed girls into adulthood, are vitally empathic creatures: hence the soft quotient of dolls, and their paraphernalia of ministering and ministered garb — a kind of gentle narcissism. Small boys, such as I once was, well, it's the clash and plunge of cars, the redounding ball, the adventuring forth, the ratification of danger, the risk of bone against bone, brittle or hardy, the mischief being chief among chiefs. But I digress …

I was first introduced to this Polish vodka, fronted with a picture of bison and bison-grass, by my maternal uncle, after a meal — in a bar in East Beirut, Achrafieh, Rue Monot, to be precise. We'd had a relatively sedate meal in the nearby Entrecote, and then, tumbling downhill towards a square recursive with bars, we entered the swankiest, the most peopled. From one corner of the crowded bar, I behind his squat magnificence, my uncle bellowed forth the demand for Zhubrowka — this uncle, worldly as they come. From that day forth, it became my drink of choice, if and when it was available, if and when I might afford it. I have drunk it, and it has drunk me, so to speak, for over a decade now, across many multi-coloured pit-stops percolating Beirut, and, betimes, in London (rarely in Spain, though once in Rome, quite unlike the Romans ...)

A maternal uncle is a maternal uncle: more than a man just to pass the baton on, the lore, the, as it happens, choicest of vodkas. Usually, he is the epitome of charisma, lent downwards from the tenderness of your mother, but banking on a more outspoken, less careful, route. Just so in my case.

So when I say those three magic words to my curt glass of ice-peopled vodka, I'm saying a kind of prayer to that mercury distillation: that it may live in me as long as it has lived in him.

(Only once has it been my honour to sup from the dregs of a bottle, by chance — upon which happening, much like the football you take home upon the event of your hatrick — and that time I was presented with the ten-inch lime-green stick of bison-grass, the equivalent of the worm at the foundation of a tequila bottle. Yet again, I digress ...)

Thus, I honour my uncle by proxy: may I be as poleaxed, but not po-faced, by this, Poland's prime artefact, as the line of kings and witty warriors whose innards have ventured, and still venture to harbour her — our commonly-kissed platinum syrup, by turns sleek or voluptuous.

As ever, but only once the sun goes down: I swivel my glass in my stony palm, and utter the great and heartfelt platitude: Zhubrowka, I love you.

A quick piece of, and in, high spirits. His uncle Walid would appreciate it. Not a bad way to start the day. Funny thing: Yusuf had discovered an optimum writerly formula for the last few years. Not the trite idea of writing while drunk: no, that inevitably led to gibberish. Rather the trick was to get absolutely plastered, and then sleep it off. The combination was like what computer-nerds called 'de-fragging.' The combination rendered the mind, or that part of it in charge of creative expression, a tabula rasa. More often than not the first thing one wrote the bedraggled morning after had a crisp freshness to it unwitnessed at other times.

After showering, Yusuf returned to his desk and found a newly received email. It was from Karim, his star-student. It was comprised of only one curt line, and there was a Word document attached. Karim's message simply said: 'I can't hide it anymore.'

Yusuf downloaded the document. Began to read ...

The Intensities and the Parentheses:
Being Extracts from the Diary of a Young Man,
Exasperated

Went to Boheme's again last night. The barman is a tall Spaniard with a striking and very masculine hook-nose. Pleasantly unassuming in the way I have found barmen can be. I like him. I ask him questions sometimes and he answers them simply. The waitress, the main waitress, the one I noticed when I first came — she beguiles me. Spidery in aspect, she looks like she harbours some special poison for rude customers. She doesn't smile when she gives me my drink. She does it, as it seems she does everything, deadpan. She makes everything around her seem absurd, myself included, but without any effort. She's a neutral counter in the place — a place of posturing — so sexy, I think.

My first drink, inevitably awkward, I preface as gracefully as possible with the lighting of a cigarette in the best way I know. The head downfaced sceptically, the left palm curved and bunched, shielding the lighter — virile — a grimace expressing distaste at the whole action. With me it has to be this way. I am like a dog — K and B never stop calling me 'the dog' for quite other reasons — marking his territory. As I admire the ashtrays, small, shallow, perfectly round glass dishes whose rims protrude thickly like labia.

At the bar two men in their thirties shout each other drinks. They are clearly South Africans visiting Beirut, because my ears are insulted by the harsh scratching of Afrikaans, which sounds like violent cursing to me. But the miracle of the thing is that every so often they slip imperceptibly into Cockney. And so the curses are followed by burlesque snippets such as: "but wosn't she laahvely!" At the far end of the bar a youngish Pakistani guy named Iqbal, I met him last week, is wearing light blue jeans and a white shirt whose overlarge collar protrudes from the neck of a salmon-pink cashmere pullover. He owns a restaurant that specialises in exotic curries, serving horse and camel among other things. We have everything in Beirut. The waitress, I noticed, has taken a dislike to him. Every time she brings a drink she serves it and then swiftly turns her back to him — a sharp, almost military swivel on the toes — as if surreptitiously to squirt poison into it from between her athletic bum cheeks. Effortlessly, she projects a kind of power and presence decidedly unromantic, pagan and austere. By turns salty, peppery.

Anyway, K and B dropped by later and we laughed a little.

***

God, make me good, but just not yet. Augustine: fool. No one can be forced to be good. One is or one isn't. Right, yes, one can be coerced, violently at times, into being right. But good? No, I am not good.

S is telling me not to worry. He says I should be happy. Yes, I say, if it were just me I would be happy. But there are other people in this world. Hell is not other people. Sartre was an idiot, a performing, dancing seal when he wrote that. Hell, as almost everyone knows, is the absence of other people: the failure, the sterile lack of other people making impact, helping to contribute. No man is an island. A cliché has avuncular integrity. It indulges you in the obvious, in common sense. And yet the tentacles I spread seem to create impassable screens. People are kept at a distance; I am kept at a distance. It's horrible panting inarticulately under the suffering cumulous of a cliché.

R thinks I'm gay, but I don't think I am. I like to think I'm like what the more astute critics think of Henry James: checked by a wound. Nowadays they would say that I am trying to recompense the loss of my mother's all-engulfing mantel. Pre-Oedipal they would call me. That is why I feel enchanted by Rome. My fear of the vagina has driven me to Rome: *ego te absolvo: credo, credo in Newmanum.* No, but really, why did God make such a tender delicate organ so bloody complicated? Ropes and pulleys, symbology, cryptic passwords you must whisper to take effect, invisible buttons ... these dregs of adolescence haunting me, crippling me. They will say then that that is further proof. But I haven't the patience to argue ... and anyway I have slept, admittedly often ineptly, with many prostitutes.

But am I superficial? I love beauty, I love image, I love form. But then it has always seemed to me that superficiality is only the lack of appreciating the innards, the essences of things. Material things have insides. A gourmet loves good food because he knows what it is, for itself. One can love a beautiful, an interesting face, the lascivious curves, the fleshly opulence of buttocks ...

... I want to be clear, crystal here. I want to spread myself flat against the page. Not so close, but enough to comfort it with style without being meretricious. A space to flow, to grace the language.

I don't hate myself; surely I'm beyond that. I hate my actions, but I love myself. That is the hope anyway.

***

I despair almost at my hysterical twaddle. Ignore, please, the frail scent of grandiosity. Anyway, S introduced me to his girlfriend last night, again. I had met M only once before. As we greeted her I reminded her immediately of the beautiful burgundy number she wore at L's wedding (a year ago). I couldn't help it: her pretty eaglet face was inseparable in my mind from the eloquent curves gliding as if on silk or ice up and down that dress. I can't help shocking a little with comments just one notch out of place. She took it well though. In fact one of the things that I noticed about her was not only that she possessed an insatiable quantity of poise and grace, but that it would somehow jar if she took anything badly. Not docile, but pliant to the right degree, touching perfectly the sweet but subtle notes of desirable femininity. And of course she has long athletic legs to die for ... My mother says I need a girlfriend. I do. I tell her I need someone with all the pluses of her sex, but without any of the minuses. I need a lithe thinking puma, not a chuckling hen. I need, I need, yes, that's bloody why!

K has an ugly girlfriend, D. I feel for him. Pale creature, she looks like she's wasting from some anachronistic illness. I keep telling him to pack her off to the Alps. She's insipid, parasitic. She, also, thinks I'm gay. In fact, for some obscure reason, all my friends' girlfriends think I'm gay. I actually have an inkling why. There is a hideous girl known to us all, a mutual acquaintance, who first bethought herself wise and intuited my inversion. She is a short, nefarious-looking elf, on the witchy side. I can't stand her. Her voice is a nasal monotone, droning without point like a housefly and occasionally alighting on your nerves and tweaking them cloyingly. Sickly bitch. I like to think of her as the human, barely, equivalent of cinnamon. Treacherous as cinnamon. She spread the rumour, I'm sure. Syrian whore ...

B's girlfriend, like B himself, is an angel. She may indeed think the same of me, but I forgive her. At any rate, she keeps it to herself, which I appreciate. She is a chipmunk, a beautiful dun-haired chipmunk. B himself is heroic, balanced. He has all the attributes: dedicated, strong, handsome, courageous, tender-hearted, forgiving, a blessing to the world. Together, Y and B are like two serene clauses of a beatitude: sublimely implying each other. Here, at last, I have a noble sentiment. Bless them ...

***

I can't seem to get my mind off that bitch, N. She has a boyfriend now. Short, comically short, just like her. I hope they have short children. I shouldn't let the thought of her bother me, but it irritates. There's nothing wrong with being gay. I would like to be quite clear about that: the insult is not there. It is in being misrepresented. To have something so fundamental to one's identity as one's sexuality questioned! I was so bloody furious two nights ago that I phoned my special mini-cab and demanded he take me to the brothel in Jounieh. I will not go into details.

B and Y took me to dinner last night. It was delightful as ever, but sometimes I feel like a third wheel. I have always felt that with B and his girlfriends. I remember way back when — when we were, as now, blood brothers — the lovely E. I think she has gone downhill since, from what I hear. But in those days she was magnificent. A peach, a princess. I enjoyed her company and B didn't seem to mind my tagging along. In fact, towards the end of school I went out with her best friend, L, for a short while anyway. L had big, maternal tits. I enjoyed squeezing them. But, going back now, I think it was from her that I derived this minor fear of vaginas, vaginas one is responsible for that is. What I mean is, what I'm trying to say, is that it doesn't matter when you are faced with someone, like a whore, who you don't give a farthing for, who won't hold you responsible mentally if you fail in any way to work it right. (I try anyway.) But I remember, one night, trying to go down on L, in the dark, it was pitch, pitch black, and surely missing wildly. I couldn't tell what was what!

Where exactly do they pee from? I fumbled about, took one swift whiff of the thing, and made a sharp exit, demanding a blow-job, which wasn't like me, but I was on the defensive, feeling at its acutest the metaphysical aloneness of each of us in this bloody accursed world. But then, as if the Gods were in the mood to mock, I couldn't get it up, and not only couldn't I get it up, but my dick shrivelled to its most infuriatingly insignificant. It was the nerves of course and I can laugh about it now.

But now that I think of it, it was Db I think; that's where it probably started. A barmaid I took out to dinner and lied to pathologically. I took her to a club later and fingered her clitoris (by accident) through her jeans. I was of course a perfect gentleman throughout the night, something I am sure she wasn't used to. When I eventually drove her back to her flat (drunk of course) she asked me in. I hesitated, naturally, but eventually made the decision. I had the heart for it then. We were lying on her bed, making out — I have always been fantastic at this: I have rhythm — and then we got naked. She started to, well, you know, doing something quite surprising and exciting at the same time, and then she asked me if I had a condom. I did, but in the car. So we slept on it, after I made her promise that we could do it when we woke. It was my first time, you see. I woke up raging, went down to my car, got the condoms and stormed back to the flat. I think, in my wiser moments, that she was already disappointed by then and was just humouring me out of innate sweetness. Luckily, as I say, I was raging. Unfortunately, however, it turned out I didn't know how to put a condom on, ripping two, flustered and furious with myself, successively. How in God's name could I be stumped by something so prosaic? I am, I keep telling myself, an imbecile.

She responded — in retrospect, I don't know

how she could have forgiven me — by telling me she was on the pill, and that we could fuck raw. So we did. And I can say that I enjoyed it tremendously, the bounciness of it all. But then something, inevitably, happened to ruin what I felt to be a triumph of the will. Being inexperienced, once I had relieved myself, I had pulled out immediately, creating one of the most disgusting — aurally, imaginatively — noises I have ever heard. A pussy fart. A pussy fart ... something from which the senses and the mind, the whole of matter and of sprit together in one thunderous chorus revolt against. The sound withers and any human person in the vicinity is struck for a freakish moment by a debilitating shame. I was momentarily paralyzed in horror. But she showed adequate remorse for it, and I was grateful enough to her for letting me have sex, that I let it go. But the sound still reverberates garishly through my eardrums now and then.

***

A little of K. He is pale, auburn haired, with sea-green eyes punctuated by specks of beige that have a tendency to be blood-shot. He is impudently petulant at times and will have his way. We, his friends, humour these bouts of authoritarianism, knowing it just to be his particular form of self-expression. He is ludicrously hygienic. He wears gloves when he travels by service and makes sure the least possible percentage of his body touches the seat, which has given him a back problem. He has been known, I myself have seen him do it, to offer chewing gum to interlocutors whose breath smells. He does not inform them directly that if they refuse he will bring the conversation to an abrupt end, but insinuates it with a pained expression of courtesy. He preys on their shame.

But he is not humourless. His humour, while at times large and warm, is not ribald. It hasn't that happy ruddy quality. It is more effeminate, set off by minute comic readings of details: a finely worked analogy to describe the way a piece of food tastes, the mental attitude of a tree, the way a duck feels upon being gang-raped. While thus dilating with a mischievous grin spread from ear to ear he will pick apart the air between his fingertips, as if pealing from it the consecutive layers of his story. His laugh is an infectious cackle, a modest kah-kah-kah. Our relationship is based on mutual understanding, a ticklish taste and a tendency to hyperbole.

***

There is another K. I will call him –K: a consummate weasel. My main objection to him is that he is ever trying to prove himself, a mirage. He has no girlfriend and I think I know why. Once, S, K, B and myself were sitting round our regular poker game of old, discussing the future whimsically. We pictured for ourselves each other's future wives, a game I delighted in. B would have someone eminently feminine, his queen. K, a comedienne. S, the nurturing sort. And me, well, they said she would walk barefoot down the aisle, a hippy type. But then we speculated about –K — we all recognize the weasel in him (he cheats at poker) — and the problem was that we couldn't for the life of us picture his future wife. My theory is, has always been, that he lacks a self. Because he is always something other, trying to be something other than real, it means there is no real 'other' in his universe. Lacking a bounded and integral self, the whole world becomes, in the most infantile way, a projection of oneself.

–K also, I suspect, thinks I'm gay. I know,

I shouldn't even bother with this, but I will, on principle. The other night we all of us went to a nightclub for K's birthday. It was supposed to be one of the most exclusive places in Beirut. But I found it ugly. Just one large oblong monstrosity in poor taste, if one is still allowed to have taste in a consumerist universe gone mad. The music was good though, and I was dancing from the first, shaking my ass with passion. As I say, I have rhythm. I noticed a Dutch girl dancing by herself near our table. I introduced myself politely and asked if I might dance next to her. I know it is not proper form in a place like that. Most guys — I don't quite understand how it works — just start dancing lewdly near a girl, grab her from behind (something, admittedly, I crave to do) and grind. I haven't it in me; somewhere I founder, pathetically. (Shame: I have the manner of a chessboard.) But I consider myself well brought-up. So I go through the absurd courtly chivalries and because I am at an expensive table with champagne, so I surmise, she is sweet to me. I find out she came with the musicians, huge and hard dreadlocked Jamaicans, who I admit have more rhythm than me. We are getting along fine, even if I feel disgusted with my sickening sweetness, my inevitable failure to produce the right edginess that will open up vistas for sexual communication. I tell myself, which I know is true, that I only need to get to know her a little, maybe take her for dinner, and then, then I could move into more predatory domains. Lacking the piercing directness of a bishop, suitably shaped, I hop around my intended like a deluded knight. However, half way through the night, –K notices how much she is beginning to like me, to think, quite correctly, how different I am from the usual posturing ego-cases. So, weasel that he is, he goes up to her while I'm not looking and whispers in her ear that I'm gay. I only heard it because I happened to be nearby and turned right at the last moment. I am always doing this. Anyway, I ignored it, as I usually do. I said nothing, but how can I deny after writing this, here, that I harbour something resentful, something spiky or blunt, either would do, towards the slimy dickhead. I have nothing against people having opinions, making judgments, we all do, but why can't they keep it to themselves? Why do they put me, always, in this awkward situation?

***

I find it difficult to write about B. He is lacking in anything forced or exaggerated. He is the most natural, the least magical, of creatures — the least socially pliant, the least mixed up with evil. Straightforward as a good piece of timber, he is the person I know most able to exist self-sufficiently. Perhaps this is the key to his good-naturedness. A brilliant human being. Brilliant at living, successful at it. He is tall, dark, incredibly handsome, with beautiful long curling eyelashes, which add a touch of prettiness to the dominant impression of virility. I have known him since I can remember to be always the lady's choice. His talk is measured and precise like his whole bearing. I admire him tremendously. K, I never fail to notice, is intensely jealous.

Y, his lady, is dear in the measure of this two-bit world. (Is that affected? I honestly don't mean it to be.) If I didn't love B so much, I would be jealous ...

They love each other but, up until tonight, I never thought they had slept with each other. Of course I could only gain this new insight from observing her. She was more possessed of him. By a happy chance grammar has caught the butterfly of this sentiment of mine mid-wing-beat. (Could be better). What I mean by this is that there is a felicity in the phrase: possessed 'of' someone. Not by him, nor possessing him. Somehow it became clear to me that somewhere inside an incipient magnetism, something all women possess in embryo form (I suppose), had been set off. Something fateful but happy. It was a pleasure to watch: to warm-hearted people such as myself the spectacle can be infectious.

Perhaps I am getting out of my depth. I cannot help but feel my inadequacy, of expression and even of understanding, when I mentally contrast my nervy articulacy with what it must feel like to be inside the relation itself. I can't help feeling that there is cruelty in me expostulating thus: if not coldness, a coolness. What do I know but words, and a feeling of helplessness? I love them both.

***

I killed a moth yesterday. I suffocated it.

It flew in fanning the air, as ever, amid manic whispers. I watched it ascend at a diagonal through the window, loop a wide one hundred and eighty degrees and then slowly descend back to the floor below the window. It limped like an invalid, hobbling upon the blades of pale blue carpet. After walking a while in pointless circles it stopped, intrigued. I grabbed an empty coffee mug, towered over it, bent low and caged it in darkness.

I saw K today. True to form our conversation was ... what's the word I want: excitable. I told him about my incident with the moth and how this morning I heard an indignant hissing from my room that was actually a string of sibilant curses in Sri Lankan. The Buddhist housekeeper was venting his fury, for the moment uncontained, upon unearthing the shrivelled body of his fellow-traveller in life. K started talking about the religious experiences of moths. He said that moths were addicts to the psychological process of conversion, hence their unhappy attraction to bright burning light. It is the need for a continuously repeated experience of trial by fire. Like Dedalus in Ulysses proving algebraically that Hamlet was Shakespeare's grandfather (or something of the sort), he told me, he would derive Bunyan from Nabokov syllogistically. His conversation then turned to some of his pet favourites — the pride and melancholy of zippers, a key-ring's nurturing side, a housefly's capacity for joy — all the while contorting his mouth as if mincing something between his fleshy lips and plucking substance from the air with his thin effeminate fingers. Listening to him is like walking into a delicatessen for the first time. He says eccentric things, imported and expensive things.

I was a regular at the restaurant we were lunching at. The staff, I'm certain, think I'm gay because I often go there alone, always in fact. Two of the waiters themselves are quite clearly gay and it is just like gay men ashamed of their sexuality to think that everyone straight is in the closet. This infuriates me.

The first one is extremely ugly. His face is quite literally rectangular. He has a wide jutting chin that pushes his mouth out of his face, giving it a simian expression. But a monkey with the airs and graces of an arthritic granny. That's what most irritates me about him. He behaves crookedly, like an old lady. Not an old coquette, an old queen, which would, I admit, bring with it colour and character, but a Victorian spinster. What's the point of being gay if you exude such feeble drabness? The second one, though overweight, is actually quite handsome. His complexion is always rose pink, but his features are nice and symmetrical. He is more on the pansy side of the homo spectrum. He has that awkwardness, that oversensitive gaucheness I have noticed in many of his type.

When I go there for a coffee or for a quick burger they serve me sardonically. I was telling K all this at lunch, taking advantage of the fact that I had support this time, and he called them, quite correctly, if a bit on the ancien régime side of things, insolent, while staring menacingly at one of the waitresses. He is a very loyal friend, but he can use the word 'peasant' too liberally sometimes.

***

The copula attack me with a curse. The untimely harrowing of harpies begins, judgments flailing dangerously about me left, right and centre, commentaries, blurred, whizzing and mad, dissecting me and closing in like a hurricane in a nightmare. I am a lonely, infinitely vulnerable subject (he) surrounded and suffocated by this menacing and multi-voiced predicate (gay). But the proposition is false. False!

The effect, though hilariously funny in parts, was infinitely clever. He was coming out of the closet, but *via negativa*. His text was an overt bluff. Fascinatingly clever; queerly so. After an hour, rereading, he emailed Karim the following message: *'Meet me at Hemingway's (Hamra) at four o'clock. If not possible, send me a preferred time.'*

Within five minutes he received a reply: *'Four o'clock* at *Hemingway's. Yes.'*

At four o'clock, Yusuf was duly seated at the bar. As he'd expected and hoped it was still too early for other clientele. When, a few minutes late, Karim entered, he took his seat next to his prof. The latter ordered for the chap, an *Almazah*. Both men sipped their respective drinks in a kind of uncanny but comfortable silence for a good five minutes. Then Karim turned to the older man and said:

'So you read it?'

'Yes.'

'Your thoughts?'

'Good stuff. Clever, perhaps a little too much so. The voice is entertaining as well as effetely aestheticist. Who've you been reading?'

'A clutch of people. Have done since I was fifteen. So you think it good?'

'That's beside the point. But yes, it is. However, I thought, I mean from your short message, that you wanted to talk about life, not fiction?'

'But the two are intertwined.'

'How so: you mean it's autobiographical?'

'Well, in parts yes. But I mean the whole flamboyant performance of the pen. It's just that, a performance. Not dramatic in the sense of Austen, all show, not tell. But dramatic like an impresario. It's the tenor and timbre of the voice that's most autobiographical.'

Yusuf pondered a few minutes, then said,

'So you're saying you're of a womanly nature?'

'Quite.'

'And this is a problem: why? You fear your parents' reaction?'

'Far from it,' Karim answered, 'even if they don't know already, mine aren't the traditionalist type.'

'Then where's the dilemma? Be who you are, or who you want to be. This is a very permissive place. You're lucky you didn't land in the Gulf!'

At this point Teymour, passing by outside, spotted Yusuf. He entered and salaamed, patting Yusuf heartily on the back and asking for an introduction.

'Professor Teymour, this is Karim Faris, one of my better, if not my best student.'

'Glad to meet you. Listen Yusuf, good I bumped into

you. There's a little shindig at my place tonight, quite early in fact. Seven-ish people should be arriving. And you owe my place a visit, old man.'

Teymour left as windily as he'd entered. But the interruption had done something to Karim. When Yusuf tried to re-initiate the conversation, to get to the nub of the young man's issue, the latter was glumly silent for a while, and then, merely said:

'It's nothing. Not a problem really. Forget it.'

Yusuf protested, but Karim was putting on his jacket. 'It's on me, Prof,' he said. And, before Yusuf could put up a fight, handed over the cash to Robbie, who was idling over a newspaper at the far end of the bar.

Five minutes later, about to leave, by sheer coincidence or serendipity, one of his younger cousins entered upon espying the seated, lonesome Yusuf. Coincidence: because it was this young woman who'd recently been diagnosed with schizophrenia. And this unhappy fate: redoubled by traditionalist parents who refused to countenance the fact in an eased manner, which would better serve the plight of their daughter.

Yusuf, still distracted after the brief encounter with Karim, took a few minutes to adapt to the new conversation.

She regaled her older cousin with tales of sedation, and the lesser frequency of shouting matches in the home. The sedation was a nuisance, but she was forced to put up with it. The good news was that she was cast for a play. Never having acted, it was only recently that she'd both the urge and the guts to try her luck at mummery. It was going to be 'the bomb.' And so on. Yusuf congratulated her and was all ears for another hour, before taking his leave, and making his way — he'd just decided — to Teymour's flat: it couldn't hurt.

Too much madness, he thought, as he ambled from one end of *Hamra* to the other, was beginning to spoil the broth: as though the lit craziness and the liquid chaos of the bric-a-brac city were pouring poisons into its exemplars.

Sunday

To look at them, seated in a kind of skewed square, a parallelogram more like, you might think it possible they were cousins. To listen in to the avid chinwag of the four: well, it spelt more the taut, distinct agonies of earth, wind, fire, water. They were arguing about religion in the same hurried tones they might use to instruct the help at their various homes in the recondite ways of preparing a meal, a meal just so. One was blonde with the whitened blondeness of a seashell. One was auburn-toned, undulant waves of a thicker honey with a touch here and there of mauve. One was almond-brown with streaks of rum and vanilla. And one was veiled with a sparkling white hijab. So it was a fashionable fight.

Lara was saying, a little on the defensive, that she'd forged her own religion over the years, snippets from her grandmother of yore, snippets from her mother, recently-passed, and to unglue these, sundering snips from her quite resolutely atheist husband. At which point, Samira interjected, while briskly straightening her veil:

'But Lara, *habeebtee*, the Koran says it all. The words are not man-made. They are not fallible. They are God's inexorable, impregnable idiom. And this is why if you go from Koran to Koran over a millennium-and-a-half, and from any point of the globe across that time, you won't a find a Koran with a different letter, or even an erring accent …'

'It *is* true, I suppose,' Sara admitted, 'that any man-made writ would be breached, here or there, then or now, eventually. It's one of the lessons I learnt from my postgraduate studies in literature. Every existing sign, which means any man-made sign — if it *is* extant, positive, that is, a part of time and space — is susceptible to the infinite interpretation that is incumbent on mortality.'

'What do you mean by that?' Lara was piqued of a sudden: it might be a way to combat the thoroughbred religious, Samira, in their midst.

'Well, it's like this,' Sara explained. 'Anything that is, is susceptible to passing, to death. Right?'

One nodded, pursing her lips encouragingly; one's eyes were beginning to screw-up tightly, as she tried to anticipate the footwork of the foe. One seemed distracted by the mute news on the television in the room, unaffected by the ruckus.

'And death means the loss of the thing, whatever it is, in its own-most presence. From then on the thing, be it someone's blouse or someone's novel, is susceptible to all the infinite divisibility of time and space. I will read the word 'tree' in a book with different signification to you, however miniscule the difference. I will wear that blouse differently to you or the deceased. Even looking at the same blouse, no longer inhabited by that person you knew, will stir different stories in each of us and so on — *quite unlike* a situation, potentially at least, where the author of the words is there to say what he or she meant, quite unlike, I mean, a situation where you're too much talking to the blouse-wearing friend, to even think of what the blouse *might mean*. No, that doesn't quite work. But it's similar. I mean, what I mean is, the blouse only spurs tales in us, or does so with more gusto, when it is emptied by a death. When the person's there, you or I might think what we like, but there is, potentially at least, an "owner", and not just in a material sense, of the blouse …'

'What has this to do with the Holy Koran?' Samira said. 'What does a blouse have to do with the Holy Koran?'

Lara took up the gauntlet.

'I think what Sara's trying to say is that *if* the book were truly God's, and God's alone, it wouldn't have been revealed in material print, however sublime the poetry, but would have been written indelibly, indelibly in the silence that is the silence of our hearts and minds.'

'But *it is: it is!*'

'But if it is, why the need of the book?'

With a mildly hurt look, a tad vulnerable, Samira replied:

'Every child that's born, all things being equal, will grow into an adult, no? But we still, as parents, as mothers, we still take care to groom them, give them structure, and so on ... No?'

Momentarily at least, this was a winning point. Sara twisted her head upwards at a diagonal, as though trying to see how the illustration fitted into her scheme of things. Lara looked at her, then Samira, then back, then back again, like a shuttlecock between the protagonists.

The one in the group who hadn't said a word, the one wearing the chunky high heels, with beautifully cascading hair and all the paraphernalia of a different kind of grooming, now said:

'I think Samira is right. We should all love God. Yes, most definitely. Now let's stop this silly squabbling. Let's go to lunch. I've been waiting half-an-hour for you three chatterboxes to finish this futile exercise.'

Smiles, in different tones and shapes and sizes, spread, shared across the small TV-room where they sat. They'd merited the right to squabble, because wasn't it true that they were kinds of gods? Of home, of children in their care or yet to be born. Weren't they, their smiles said each to each, the bedrock of human civilization? Woman, they seemed to say telepathically, Woman was the keystone of all odysseys: they were Ithaca, eternally Ithaca. Secretly, each one harboured an unspoken suspicion that God was a She.

It was half past noon. They all stood up and filed out for lunch. It was Sushi today ...

Yusuf stirred from sleep just as the four cousins had reached this point of appeasement, and took their leave. Shards of their conversation had penetrated his half-dormancy, the door closing putting the finishing touches to his rousing. He'd had a strange dream: there was a dragon …

A dragon as he remembered them from his childhood cartoons: a tall cedar-green and corn-yellow reptile, the size of a modern-day skyscraper, towering above the human tokens of his self, his mother and his father. The dragon — smugly brandishing each of his parents in its ivory claws — put the most basic but sinister of conundrums to him. He'd a choice, either his father was to be gobbled or his mother munched. Every now and then, a snapshot from a beach of a darkly platinum sea, with black looming fins, interjected the more continuous dragon narrative. When faced again with the dragon, in a kind of uncanny blur between his four-year-old and present selves, Yusuf found himself trying to negotiate with the fantastic creature, at times articulate as his adult self, at others with a kind of childish whining. Most children would have opted for the mother to survive the ordeal: indeed Yusuf was tempted; in fact tempted beyond the norm. But he was smart, cunning even: he'd tried bargaining for a third option, and just as the gargantuan monster growled a loud *No, Never!* he'd a glimpse of a black fin veering farther (or further) inwards towards shore, a gabble of geese-like voices and then, intruding, the clunk of the front door shutting, and he was now drowsily awake …

He'd read somewhere, perhaps in Tolstoy, the theory that the whole content of one's dreams was experienced, in real time, in the last minute or moments before waking: that it was some completely contingent surrounding or happening that spurred one's dream: say, a bee buzzing near your sleeping ear. But what did sharks, dragons and gabbling geese have in common? The sharks were fearsome fins in a sea. The dragons were fiery in fiery dungeon-like lairs and caves. The geese just hobbled around in wonky circles in some farmyard or pen.

Pondering these themes, while pouring the milk on his cornflakes, Yusuf answered the ringing phone. It was his mother to say she'd left her keys behind, so that he wasn't to leave the house before she returned in an hour or so, to let her in. No skin off his back, as he lounged, slouched, still in his pyjamas, in 'his' corner of the wide foursquare living room, continuing to read Plato's *Phaedrus*. A kind of madness was the theme, that betokened by *Eros*, which was a metaphor for the centripetal use of the imagination, via the drawing-in of sometime-sundered lover and beloved. Mania, he noted, must have derived from what the introduction had highlighted: the concept of *'manikos.'*

He looked out of the wall-wide window of their plush, svelte third-floor apartment, onto Verdun Street, and watched the chock-a-block horn-hooting traffic for a moment or two — thinking how lucky he was, how unlucky ...

*

How unlucky, yes, but how lucky ...

Robbie began working at the age of seven, but only, at this early age, during summer holidays. His paternal uncle, Albert, was an artisan, a maker of bags and sacks. Briefly, Robbie had worked for him, and the workload wasn't too hard. Specifically because making his own money, however paltry, felt liberating.

'For the first time, I was able to buy friends the odd present, a Pepsi, say. And I was able to chip in to the daily household expenditure. For example, my mother's favoured mint and coffee. I still remember how elated I felt when I first brought home some goodies for my mother. She cooed, and I felt like a Prince.'

Later he worked in a sandwich shop, specializing in oven-baked savouries, such as the staple Levantine breakfast of *Mana'eesh*. Yet the owner of the shop recognized early on that Robbie was too smart to work at the stove. He was asked to watch over the till and the accounts. The owner of the place suspected Robbie's colleague, a few years older, was skimming off the top. Robbie duly noticed that this suspicion was in fact accurate. But he was on good terms with his fellow-worker.

'The owner was a real hard-case, a real asshole to my friend, so I thought I needn't inform on him: *Ha'oh*, I thought, given how he was treated, maybe a little extra money was his due.'

Later, again artisanal, he apprenticed in a barbershop. Working there let him buy his first brand new bicycle, a BMX for twenty dollars. Before then he'd been fobbed off with second, third and fourth-hand hand-me-downs.

At fourteen, he waited tables in restaurants while being enrolled, like most young teenagers in school. Until the age of thirteen he was schooled with the élite, in the Christian Teaching Institute. The yearly toll on his working class family was a hefty sum back then, as now: three thousand dollars. When he changed to the 'Providence' school the bill was only a thirty percent decrease. The problem (among mounting problems) was, having been in a more advanced system Robbie was academically a year ahead of his peers in an educational system far, far less targeted. From Providence, he moved to '*Achrafieh* Public School.'

'The school was not so bad, but I was …'

In these mid-teen years, till the age of seventeen, when he left education for good, he became depressed, turned a harsh stinging glare inwards, and took on the black mantel of self-destructiveness. This was probably the outcome, especially difficult during one's teenage years, of feeling out of place among his peers. There were times when he couldn't afford to go to school. His father would give him a thousand Lebanese *lira* a day, but the bus ride to school and back was half that, each way, leaving him penniless for other things like lunch. The majority of his peers in these schools were middle class; and they could afford nice clothes and all the other artefacts of ease, of comfort; so, while still working part-time, Robbie felt even more pressingly the ill and jilting logic of his world.

He gained weight, and under this new frightening imago, subliminally introjected the inevitable sense of alienation, ultimately, punishing himself as a way of working through what the world did on a daily basis.

'My first instinct was to hide my new-found identity, to deny.'

Such furtiveness meant stress beyond that native to the anyway-troubled period in life's course. He was a teenager, but as though a teenager compounded, squared.

At seventeen, then, he decided that 'education' was a lost cause, that it made no material difference to someone like him. In his mind, he'd given up. Being a 'Palestinian,' he felt that with all the degrees in the world he'd never be able to get on and get ahead in Lebanon.

And when he began working fulltime at seventeen, this self-punishment took on a more fully external, virulently material life. For now he had to produce CVs and fill in numberless application forms. If his first instinct was to hide and deny, that closet became hollowed in the most fundamental way. Damage became a living, moving place in the outer world. Congenitally then, he was officially a hunted person.

So he began waiting tables in restaurants. Being the youngest of the hired workers, his load was extortionate, and mule-hard. He'd to carry trays laden with all sorts, back and forth, back and forth, for ten to eleven hours in the day.

At this, his first full-time job, he'd passed an interview with the restaurant manager, a tall, authoritative, muscular twenty-year-old. The latter had asked him what kind of workload he wanted. It was Robbie who replied that he wanted as much work as possible, including extra shifts. An angry young man, filled with angst, a deeply pessimistic tunnel vision, he thought the best thing to do was to keep as busy as possible. Maybe due to the closeness of their ages, the manager asked him why, at such a young age, he wanted to foreclose all prospect of a social life and all the usual paraphernalia associated with one's teen years. Robbie, now as then, knew that what the manager was intimating was right. But he'd gotten into a rigid groove of denial and self-punishment; it was too hard, too damn hard to think himself out of the box. So that Thursday morning, when the manager asked when would he like to start, Robbie replied, *Tomorrow*.

The manager smiled ruefully, telling him to start on Monday and have fun over the weekend: there would be plenty of time for work from then on. No doubt he admired the young man's brave gusto.

'The twist in the tale though, was that for some reason this manager never bothered to ask about my nationality. The fact of being Palestinian was in this case neither here nor there ... I owe that man a lot.'

At eighteen, his elder brother, Ely, got him a job as a diamond-setter, a job which he kept for two and a half years; tellingly: artisanal again. It was commonly thought that learning this particular trade would set you up, eventually, to 'mint' your own money; it was thought that once fixed in such a career you'd be set, much like the erstwhile diamonds. He was paid roughly twenty dollars per week during this time.

'For a heavy smoker, that was a pittance. Hardly — no: not enough.'

He suffered increasingly frequent migraines from the work of peering all day down a microscope as he set diamonds into golden and silver bands. He worked from nine in the morning till midnight, and then, later, from nine till three in the morning; hardly artisanal hours. Eventually his sight suffered: both as cause of and as concomitant to the periodic headaches.

Restaurants and nightclubs became his staple work from then on, finally ending here, in *Hemingway's*.

'It's taken me eight years, eight angry, troubled years — from seventeen to twenty-five — 'till I became the Robbie, your friend, standing here before you.'

'But you're married Robbie,' Yusuf replied, 'tell me *that*

tale.'

Robbie looked at his wristwatch.

'Don't worry: no one's going to enter for another half-hour at least. For goodness sake I know the ins and outs of this place better than you! So, tell me.'

By the end of his seventeenth year, Robbie had been jailed twice — only a few days each time — for being involved in violent brawls. An angry young man, he looked for fights. To this day he looked upon those incidents as holographs of any real life; sham selves spending themselves without issue. The girl (now his wife) who'd prove prodigal spur to overcome this, his prodigal erring, didn't know him or of him as yet.

Marie-Rose was a friend of Robbie's elder brother's wife. It was the latter who set them up. Though the sixteen-year-old Marie-Rose was a beautiful and tranquil-seeming girl, evocative of all that home and safety might ever possibly intend, Robbie was too caught up in his posturing, acting the cad, the rude-boy. At their first encounter, she didn't take to him at all. So when he asked her — at the end of a night's boyish swagger and showy rendition — if he might see her again, she replied with a resolute 'No.'

But Robbie was persistent. He asked her out again two weeks later.

'Who knows what made her change her mind: perhaps she was overly wise for her age? Perhaps she thought she'd nothing to lose? Perhaps her friends egged her on?' Robbie smiled nostalgically. 'Anyway, she agreed, and we met-up at Dunkin Donuts. This time I was different.'

They talked with honesty, and made tentative gropes at the core of each to each. It was an original experience for Robbie. He felt like a gate swung open onto a wholly different, unique world, and the shock was a kind of grace. And he now ached inside with what can only be called the agony of joy.

Before escorting her home, Marie-Rose kissed him. She kissed him: her womanly sixth sense burgeoning. Instantly, Robbie emerged flourishing in a newly-minted world, in a new Spring-sprung earth, as though he'd been previously residing and dizzily spinning on a crater-filled moon. He underwent a sea change, a tipping point. Had he been twenty years older one would have called it 'a climacteric.' Now, in a sky-blue light, he was 'a normal guy,' like all the others. He had a girlfriend. He had a girlfriend!

(The same taut rite was now performed: tugging downwards on his white shirt …)

Then again, later that year he went to jail for a third time, for having smoked hashish. But the arrest was made belatedly. He'd smoked at the home of a friend. This foolhardy fellow showboated in front of the wrong guy, someone who turned out to be an insider in the employment of the police. Robbie was walking down a street when a police officer accosted him and asked for his identification documents. He was shuttled from police station to police station. In the last station before appearing in court, he was beaten by the police on the backend of verbal abuse for being a Palestinian in Lebanon. Even though Robbie's father had friends who'd some, if not much, influence with the police, they were too late: by the time the requisite phone call came through, he was already battered and bruised. After going through the formality of a court appearance he disappeared for twenty-two days.

But, canny as ever, Robbie could think on his feet. By sharing his mother's sumptuous homemade food and cigarettes he befriended the hardcore, much older men within the prison. His mother visited twice: once in a room where they could talk over a table, once partitioned. Her tears, both times, were like a hot wrenching on the steeled seventeen year-old. He too wept, profusely. Shame mounted shame.

When he got out, still an item with the lovely Marie-Rose, he turned defensive, or, better, self-defensive in a new way. He felt the shame of what he'd gone through redoubled in the lamp and the mirror of his young and perfect love. He told her that his jail experience meant that her parents would surely prevent her from seeing him. Not only was he a Palestinian Christian (to which, much earlier she'd replied, succinctly: 'I don't give a damn!') but now he'd a bona fide criminal record. His reputation, he felt, would follow him like a gargantuan stink.

She hugged him. She kissed him. 'I don't care, I don't care,' she said. And then, beaming from ear to ear, she'd said: 'But Robbie: you smell.'

In the immediate moment, all seemed well. And yet, his self-defensive fears were not too far off the mark. For Marie-Rose's parents pressured and urged her to end the relationship. Their attitude to the young Robbie, while understandable, was skewed. Once on an outing to the beach, while Marie-Rose was snacking with Robbie, her mother whispered to her to 'be careful: he's probably put hashish in your *Mana'eesh*.' Proud as ever, Robbie feigned ignorance, but was, quite naturally, wounded.

Though they did indeed break up briefly, within a week of separation they were back together. That week rendered both of them desperate, urgent. So, in secret, they got back together. Cunning, in the good way only first love can be, Robbie used to walk Marie-Rose from *Achrafieh* where she studied to *Bourj Hammoud*, where she, like he, lived. That was the daily slot of time when love gained its close momentum.

'It was the only part of the day when her parents were unsuspecting. They knew the time it took for her to walk home. It was the one hour in the day which was hidden from her parents' eyes. Our friendship deepened until it was full and overflowing — we were in love.'

Verily: Capulets, Montagues, Yusuf mused. *Hemingway's* was just beginning to be peopled by stray clientele. Yusuf decided to stay off the drinks and so he left: briefly humbled by his friend's tale, on this, the day of rest.

Monday

'**What do you think are the** meanings evoked or invoked by the very title: "Mr Sludge, The Medium"?' Yusuf was teaching Browning at his best this morning.

Cynthia put her hand up, and answered: 'The idea of being compromised, in the middle of things, as though in mud.'

'Good,' Yusuf answered. 'There is that. For instance, as we saw, he starts *in medias res*. Good. But about the idea of "medium" … Anyone?'

Cynthia answered again. 'It refers to the spiritualism.'

'Yes. But also there is what in narratology is called the 'reflector'. Can anyone guess what this means?'

No one put their hand up.

'A reflector is a character *through whom* we as readers are permitted to enter the tale; to a certain extent, for all their action in the tale, in this case a dramatic monologue, they are functionally passive, and reflect for us.'

Cynthia put her hand up again. 'Isn't that what Keats meant by "negative capability"?'

'Precisely, Cynthia, well done! Yes, Keats invented this term to explain the genius of Shakespeare. But tell us more, Cynthia.'

'It's as you say, like in Browning here: the character is like a mirror for us readers. I think Shakespeare was like a medium because he was the kind of genius who was universal, who was able, like a medium, to reflect his age, right?'

'Exactly. And not only his age, but all of civilized human history. No one, anywhere, I believe, can be left untouched by Shakespeare's imagination. Good. So "negative capability."' Yusuf chuckled deprecatingly, telling his students that, after Cynthia's contribution, they'd gone beyond the bounds of what he'd wanted to teach. But that was a good thing.

'Good. So we've the notion of being a medium in the spirit-seer sense and in the narratological sense. Anything else?'

The classroom was quiet.

'I mean: is there any other level upon which the medium mediates or reflects? No? Well, think of it like this: he's not only a medium for his special-pleading, not only a medium caught as a fraud, but there are very significant ways in which his literal story carries within it a figurative subtext, for the purposes of the poet, Browning. For example, when he invokes the idea, as one of many of his excuses, of being like a 'romance' writer, or an actor, or a poet, perhaps he's reflecting the emergent sense in Browning's time of a new aesthetics, that the dichotomy of true and false, fiction and reality, is not as hard-and-fast as all that. Can anyone think of examples of this kind of Late Romanticism in the second-half or indeed fourth-quarter of the nineteenth century?'

Cynthia put her hand up again. 'Oscar Wilde's "The Decay of Lying."'

'Good. Yes. The *unimportance* of being earnest. Good.' Half the class laughed, picking up on the reference, the other looked on, enviously. Then the bell rang. As they filed out, Yusuf asked Cynthia to wait behind. They'd five minutes before the next class arrived and he asked her what ideas she might have about making up for the classes she'd missed. He hadn't planned on mentioning her father's request. But he decided to do so; they were in private. When he mentioned that her father had had a word with him, she flinched, then grimaced. He eased her worries and said there was no question of '*wasta*.' That he was right to mention it. They agreed that he'd give her a week-and-a-half beyond the deadline for the final research paper, in which time she was to produce both the latter and the two most substantial pieces of missing work from earlier in the semester. She thanked him, now in a plucky mood, and exited the class with a pronouncedly boyish swagger.

After lunch, Yusuf had an office-hour, to which no student turned up. Just about to leave his office, five minutes to go, Karim bumped into him at the doorway, asked if he might have a minute.

'Why of course, Karim. Yes, our chat the other day was disrupted.'

'I just came to say that I'm sorry. That I was temporarily insane. I'm not that way, in fact.'

Yusuf was troubled, but tried to hide his mystification under a veneer of ease and breeziness.

'Yes?'

'I mean I just wanted you to know. I'm sorry for having troubled you.'

'Listen, Karim, if there's anything I can ever do …'

'Please don't worry professor. I'm fine. And thank you for your understanding.'

He turned and left. Yusuf stood in the doorway of his office, puzzled. 'Till Teymour turned the corner and slapped him on the back and said, 'Quite an evening the other night? Ay? Told you I'm a good host. Now you know, old man.'

'Yes. I enjoyed it,' Yusuf said, snapping out of his puzzlement.

'And what do you think of that Randa? She stayed latest, last. I've got to tell you …'

Yusuf put his hand up to curb his friend's wagging tongue.

'Another time. I've class.' He lied, but it worked: Teymour headed off on his way, whistling a tune.

In fact, Yusuf had a free hour. Instead of having a nap in the departmental lounge, he went to the see the Chair, a gay man himself, he believed. He wasn't particularly close to the man, but there was respect between them and they'd always been civil to each other. He wanted the benefit of his experience.

After waiting fifteen minutes with the departmental secretary (sultriest, most lava-like of women), Dr. James Selby opened his door and ushered Yusuf in.

'What can I do for you Dr. Ghaleez?'

'Well, it's about a student of mine. A very brilliant one in fact. I'm a little at a loss …'

'You, or him?'

'Well me, but I think anyway because he too.'

'And so what can I do?'

Yusuf hadn't thought it through. How exactly does one broach a subject like this?

'Well. It's about his identity. I mean this young man seems a little confused. And I know something of this subject. I just wanted to take your advice, as … as a gay man …'

'Who: you or me?' And he smiled widely.

Yusuf had bitten the bullet.

'Well I'd always thought you were a gay man. What I mean to say is, I thought it was common knowledge. And that …'

'I see,' the Chair now said, gesturing for Yusuf to calm down from his evident fluster. 'So you think this young man is homosexual. And?'

'Well, that's just it. I met with him on the weekend and he said as much. But then today, only two days later, he told me it was all a mistake, a mix-up. Well I thought, I mean, I think it a little strange. And you never know with these brilliant kids, what kind of poison ivy they make of their feelings. The smarter they are …'

'The more complicated?'

'Well, yes …'

'So. Would you like me to have a chat with him?'

'No. Of course not. There's a good reason I haven't mentioned his name. I'm not even sure I've done the right thing in running it by you.'

'No harm done.' Dr. Selby seemed keen to end the

conversation. 'My door's always open for you Dr. Ghaleez. Now, if you'll excuse me, I've a long list of meetings and appointments. Good afternoon.'

'Good afternoon.' Yusuf had wanted to say that he'd always thought that one's sexual orientation was the equivalent of having, say, short or long hair. But a minute later, he was glad he hadn't. It smacked of protesting too much, and would have implied some sort of subterranean homophobia. Dr. Selby wasn't stupid, after all.

*

That evening, Yusuf waited for his (still living) maternal uncle to arrive. The latter had given him directions to a new joint he'd recently discovered on the other side of *Hamra*. Yusuf had arrived ten minutes early. Which, given his uncle's peccadilloes meant, in real time, half an hour early.

Near one corner of the joint, the owner (a woman with a fine balance of flair and sense) sat at a game of *towleh* with the younger half of the barkeep team. Every few seconds, he extemporized on his shitty luck, using betimes the numbers one to six of the dice as tokens for expletives in the arena of Fortune (*Naseeb*) or luck, shitty luck (*Huzz-khara*). This young chap seemed together-enough on the whole; the other half of the bar-keep team was, as far as Yusuf's intuition suggested, a few months shy of a nervous breakdown. One had the peacefulness of the idle and uncaring, Yusuf mused, the other of the taut and suspicious mummer, as though for all the surface-calm, there were dormant torrents to rough up the fish, odd and even, little and large.

The music was vintage *Tarab*: collated chanting and the odd whiff of impresario; sorrowful in each other's vicinity; neighbours, each to each, without a neigh. It occurred to Yusuf that if the Arabs are good at anything together — and par excellence the Lebos — it was being miserable. It's the only unison they were able to muster, in their staple world of mustard and vinegar and lemon. Like infants they could only express love by hate, pillow by dagger, linen and silk in the franker language of whipcord and hairshirt.

A couple, not yet elderly, but not in the spring of their lives either, entered. They sat themselves at the table just in front of him, began to chatter with melodrama, but, to be fair, the melodrama of the honest, not that of bad faith. The grand gestures in body and word seemed native, not put-on, not puppetry. By turns, in the far corner, a deuce of adolescent girls were pedantically wonky with their youth. Yusuf, to even his own surprise, was drinking diet Seven-up, his Polish vodka a wailing refugee, the burly bison soaking himself in some other, possible world. Unlike me, Yusuf thought, amusing himself, God is getting pissed with some part of his toe or toenail.

The place was cool, in dimly-lit vermilion. It had the air of a boutique, a scholar among bars, with none of the pretension. The place was dubbed 'Madam Om', referring to the legendary Egyptian songstress *Um Khulthum*. And that name mothered the inkling of a one-time sage, her hair up in a jet-black, bird-like bundle. She'd the hips, not of the female viscera, but of a more hale period in Arab history, that of his father's spring (Yusuf extemporized, treading boards in his mind), the era of Nasser, and hope: the grand awakening south hurrying like torpedoes, but unbeknownst, into a fast array of despotisms. As it happened, they, the Arabs, had ventured too far, too fast. But in that amber-gilded moment, O, the eyes dripped with honey, like the honey-hair of his mother; their bulbous hearts weren't the red of blood but of ruby. Their spring, quite unlike the present one, was green, unescapably green — green, as the emeralds of his mother's eyes ...

Interrupting these thoughts, Yusuf's uncle Walid arrived. After grandiloquently greeting the owner he seated himself opposite his nephew, and ordered, braying above Yusuf's protest, two *Zhubrowka's*. When the madder side of the barkeep team said that, unfortunately, they were temporarily bereft of that Polish delicacy, Walid ordered a couple of *Araks*, after cursing the guy playfully.

'Ah ... you reach an age *ya khalee...*' his uncle was

saying an hour later, the older and the younger man by now tipsy and slurring. 'You reach an age when you regret not having married, not having kids. I mean, sure, yes, I had my fun, but you reach an age …'

Yusuf had heard large and wondrous tales from his youth of the sort of mischief and fun this magical man had gotten up to. An art-dealer in Paris in the seventies and eighties, he'd pulled off all sorts of 'capers'. There was the time he wanted to take whatever morsel of a model he was dating to some highly exclusive restaurant. So, he'd call up the place and pretend to be the secretary or the good friend of the great French movie star, 'Belmondo'. Immediately, he'd been accommodated and with the best table in the house. Then, seated with said morsel, every half-an-hour, the *maître-d'* politely stepped up to ask after the great man. Uncle Walid checked his watch, with a sincere and agonizing look, and said that he must have been caught up in traffic, or some sundry excuse. And so on, until they'd finished.

'It was an excellent ploy, *ya khalee*. Full-proof in more than one way. Not only did I get the best table in the house, but the — forgive me, but I like the word — *chutzpah* of pulling off such a caper was just as sexy and alluring for the chick as any real connection with the great actor. Ah …'

'But you get to an age …'

By this time, Yusuf was so enamoured of the telltales that the whole moral of the story, 'that you get to an age,' was irrelevant as some hermetic footnote.

When Yusuf got home that night, he found another email from Karim.

Tuesday

Karim's message was short: it merely said, again, thank you to Yusuf, for taking the time to talk to him. But by noon the next day, the news was spread across campus and it seemed to Yusuf that he was the last to know. He'd entered his class and found all the girls in tears, and some of the boys. He asked Latifa immediately and she replied, blubbering among the words, that Karim had killed himself the night before. He'd jumped off the balcony of his parents' fifth-floor flat, to his death. Yusuf felt burdened beyond the staple of grief. The President pronounced the rest of the afternoon as a time for mourning and reflection.

It didn't make much sense. With the email, the curt email he'd sent late the night before, he'd attached two parts of a short story set in London. It evinced a light touch. He'd sent it especially to Yusuf, not only on the face of things because he'd made use of his name, but also because he knew Yusuf had grown up in London. It was one of the first things he'd told his students, when introducing himself, though it was obvious from his accent. Karim, it seemed, had drawn on a recent holiday there, this just-passed Christmas. Feeling terribly saddened, Yusuf went back to the story. There must have been some kind of subtext. He sat in his office, a strange quiet reigning across the campus, and read, and re-read.

1
After Bathsheba

If his neighbour was, of all things, an ice-skating judge, then perhaps Yusuf had the right to spend his spare hours reading outdated arguments — deployed in a manner distinctly after the wake and pyre of Plato — in the well-hung, or well-hanging, corpus of Saint Augustine.

When that Saint stole a peach for the sake of stealing a peach, not from need, not even from desire, he condemned himself ... Ultimately, this was, it now occurred to Yusuf, how the Saint depended, or came to depend ...

And the painting in striated blues that hung behind his now seated figure, a painting in some no-man's land between empathic representation and schizoid abstraction, was either well-hung, or not so: depending ...

Again, he pondered the newly-acquired knowledge about the neighbour next door. He wondered how one got into the business of being an ice-skating judge. Did it entail having once been a native and coursing slicer of the epic ice oneself? Or was it something one might study at university, or some bestial perversion of such?

Yusuf sipped his beer, and swallowed a burp moments later. For these thoughts threatened sheer depths of infinity. And everyone knows how serious infinity is: indeed, infinity was a space where none might fart.

Yusuf sipped his beer again. It occurred that the pregnant build-up at the tip of his colon might only be gas; but there was always the risk that it was the real thing. He dithered and the image of shagging his sister from behind distracted him momentarily. No, he decided, it was worth the risk. He followed through ...

***

The next morning, Yusuf was woken by the shrill sound of his doorbell. Nadim, recently-acquired as a friend, rushed passed him and gunned straight for the bathroom, subsequently emitting wide-sounding grunts of relief and satisfaction as he emptied his bladder.

'You do know, Yiz, that there are two huge black men superintending these buildings?'

'Yes,' Yusuf replied, trying not to yawn, 'I've known it for the three years I've lived here. And who are we to judge men with well-nigh obsidian phalli?'

'Don't be a clown. What I was going to say was that one of them threatened me on my way in.'

'What did he say?'

'He said that he didn't recognize me, and when I said I was your friend, he gritted his teeth and swore under his breath.'

'Which doesn't amount to an insult: perhaps he merely thought you were a boyfriend of sorts. There's been much rubble and gossip hereabouts insinuating that I'm a queer, and a raging one at that.'

'That's because you book and sleep with whores on a weekly basis.'

'How does it follow?'

'Well, any regular guy might do it as a one-off, but when it becomes your whole *modus operandi*, people may begin to speculate. It was one of the first things you told me about yourself. You should be more discreet.'

'I play checkers, then, they play chess.' And Yusuf smiled inwardly at the felicitous phrasing he'd just chanced upon.

'It's not a good idea,' Nadim said. 'You trust so much in the goodness of people, you end up mistrusting yourself and them. You do it to yourself.'

'Yes, well, that's what you get from such a loving, affirmative upbringing: one can still lay claim to angelic status though supping each evening in hell.'

Nadim scowled.

'On another matter, did I tell you my sister is engaged to be married?'

'No,' Yusuf replied, 'but I expected as much. You reek this morning of a type who's sister is to be taken and ravished in wedlock.'

'What does that mean?'

'It means you're visiting me this morning at such an early, ungodly hour that there must be something, something new you want to tell me, and as I know you live with your sister, and don't currently have a paramour, and as you always spend half your time talking to me about the shenanigans of said sister, and as I'm a bit of a visionary and a seer and a Jeremiah …'

Nadim, distracted by the painting of striated blues, pointed at it and said: 'I haven't seen that before. What is it? It's quite evocative.'

Turning to look at the painting, Yusuf curled his lips in consideration of how to articulate a neat exposition of what it was or was about. And then: 'So Victoria's getting hitched. Good. May she have Titans for sons and seamless dolls for daughters. And may the first wear dresses and the latter pinstriped suits.'

Waving away the flippancy with pursed lips, Nadim was still peering intently at the painting. He said, 'It reminds me of a dream I once had.'

'How old were you?' Yusuf asked, poised, grinning.

'Oh, eleven or twelve.'

'That's about right then.'

'Right for what?'

'Well, for the transition into the perversity of adolescence.'

A silence ensued, while Yusuf put the finishing touches on his outfit for the day. Both young men left the flat and headed towards Holland Park, where they'd a dutiful appointment with some duly-readied marijuana. Their intents were big with the idea of frittering the day, 'till the evening draped the sky in platinum and gunmetal, 'till there was no more sluggish drug with which to fiddle their crisp minds.

***

There were tears in Yusuf's eyes. Any onlooker might think they welled from sorrow but it was honed, plosive laughter. Before him was the unparalleled humbug of a gay man, like some circus entertainer, trying to hide and downplay the mushroom of his erection. His partner, evidently, had just given him a wet French kiss before standing up to go to the toilet of the brasserie. Yusuf was tickled. Maybe he too should grow a Dali-like moustache and cut and style his hair in some outrageously tasteless way. That was the paradox of the gays: each one, like all the rest, was or tried to be an exception to his species. It was a sort of Cretan Liar's paradox. Swallowing his mirth, but still glowing with bonhomie, he decided to engage with the queen.

'I too am a gay,' he began.

'Excuse me?'

'I said: I too am a friend of falafel. But well peppered. And with what one can of salad to give moisture and added texture.'

The gay man winced, at a loss. So Yusuf continued.

'I have always wondered about people like

you, your burly boyfriend, and of course myself. Is it true to say that we're constitutionally frightened of growing up and risking real emotive engagement with the other? Is it true we pick a specimen of our own sex because we're in-built chicken-shits?'

Gathering himself now (erection either turned fallow, or subtly muzzled), the gay man retorted in a high-pitched and haughty voice, 'Actually, it's not true. All my boyfriends have been very different to me. Actually, I avoid any guy who's mirror-like to me. But then you know that.'

'Cheers to that: *santé*,' Yusuf said chirpily, while lifting his glass of Polish vodka in a fat and ceremonious way. Meanwhile, the gay man's boyfriend returned from the loos.

'Where are you from?' Yusuf asked the evidently Semitic couple.

'Israel,' the second, muscle-bound man replied.

'Ah, and I am Lebanese. I once — this was before I realized the heft of homosexuality in me — I once had an Israeli girlfriend. No, I had some opportune and extremely spicy, minutes-long sex, against the wall, with an Israeli lady officer in the Tel Aviv airport. She'd raven hair, and I was a type of such beauty back then …' He lied extremely well.

'We are not Zionists,' the first man said.

'And I, though I was born Sunni and though both my parents were and are rabid atheists, I presently approach Catholic Christianity, but have a native penchant for the paratactic unction of Judaic utterance. The Psalms now …'

'We're gay,' the first one said, 'but that doesn't mean we thrive on rarefied and cultivated conversation.' At this the first gay man opened his mouth on the verge of protesting, clearly having something at stake being risked by his boyfriend's put-down. But the burly chap waved his partner swiftly into silence, as though not wanting the latter to ruin his own (their own) repulsing gambit with this homophobic homosexual.

But Yusuf found it easy to defuse the situation. It was in his nature to be peaceable after a testing sortie. With an ingratiating smile he slowly retrieved the cocked archers from the turrets of his tower. He laid the drawbridge down across the shit-hued moat.

'Gentlemen,' he now said, 'a drink on me if you will?'

They looked at each other, smiled and said, 'Why not?'

'So: what is it you guys are drinking: dirty martinis?'

'No. I'll have a beer and he'll have a gin and tonic.'

It occurred to Yusuf, making an inward inference, to offer a quip here. But he was able to restrain himself. He told the gay waiter (to tell the gay waitress) to get the drinks for his fellow gay acquaintances.

'Thus, gents, we've shared what de Quincey once dubbed, "a jewelly parenthesis of pathetic happiness". It's been a pleasure. But now I must take my leave of you, and the subtle merriment of your affections, and the nuanced niceties of your potential defections.'

The thickset gay man and the scrawny gay man both raised their glasses once more, clink-clinked in high and pinkly unison, as Yusuf sauntered off, swaying his hips with purpled emphasis ...

Getting onto a bus, he rhetorically asked the Kensington air: 'Now, where is my Bathsheba?'

***

On the bus journey home, some virtual Bathsheba in his mind, Yusuf found himself more than once straying onto the lush terrain of thoughts about his mother, the first woman, his sacred circle.

She was a deeply passionate woman, but she was not dramatic. The flamboyance of her son was epigone and artefact of her containing poise. The surety she'd given him made him take on the nifty, shifty garbs of the chameleon, while never being lost or dispersed in whatever role he felt it incumbent on him to don.

Mariam was an atheist, like her husband. True, she was wont to remark that religion had done as much good as it had patently wrought wrongs, but she thought God was an evident stopgap, a token, which man, with protean ingenuity, had placed above him to plug the various lacunae of his knowledge and of his dithering will. Fear and ignorance were the ministering angels at the birth of the One God, not to mention the various pantheons, absurd with the absurdity of Man, only Man. She was fond of quoting a phrase that had once struck her with the ring of pithy truth, from some novel: 'Men are men; but Man is a woman.' Her favourite author (whom she'd made Yusuf read at the age of eleven) was Jane Austen. The two women, separated by centuries, had the same biting temperament; Mariam called a spade a spade.

So when Yusuf arrived for dinner, it being his younger brother's birthday, she stared a beeline at him with her deep-set emerald eyes: a look part-inquisitive, part-accusatory. She'd a hypnotic effect. Yusuf rarely laughed with his mother, though he could, especially of late, bellow with his father. She now said:

'Said is waiting for you. You're late. And what's this?' She pointed at a heart-shaped sludge-brown stain on his grey shirt.

'I spilled some coffee: the bus ride was a bit bumpy.'

'How many times have I told you, don't buy drinks from those modern coffee-shops. A waste of money and a waste of money doubled. I've told you, most of them donate proceeds to Israel.'

Yusuf looked a bit abashed. As ever, his rejoinder fell on flat ears. 'Mum, you named me Joseph before I was even born.'

Mariam pursed her lips and made a derisive clucking sound with her tongue, as if to say, 'Don't start …' Her honey-auburn hair, a kind of lioness's mane, but recently-trimmed, put her Roman features into striking relief. She was a Sophia Loren type, Yusuf had always said. While at school he'd verily boasted about his mother's good looks.

'Is Dyala coming?'

'No. Her lay-over in London was shortened by three hours, because her first flight was delayed. She just called to say that she wouldn't be able to come, have dinner, see you, Said and your father, and then get back in time for her connection.'

'Shame. I was actually thinking of her today,' Yusuf said over his shoulder as he walked into the den to find his young teenaged brother in a seemingly facile lotus position in front of the TV, and his greying father slouched in a deep crimson leather armchair, somewhere just short of snore-laden sleep. He'd added weight since the last time Yusuf had visited his parents' home in Wimbledon.

Said greeted his brother. Yusuf leant over his father and gently kissed his dozing forehead. His father slowly awoke on impact, with a momentarily baffled look, somewhere between dream and verity.

Yawning, he now said, 'Habibi. Good. Now we can eat. I don't like it that your sister can't be here. But anyway: beggars can't be choosers.' And he chuckled gently to himself. Though his father spoke fluent English, even before they'd come to London in 1975, at the beginning of the Lebanese Civil War, he took an almost profane pleasure in using pat proverbs and stock phrases, even when the situation didn't quite require or ally with it. On the phone, part of his touching politesse found itself always articulated in phrases like 'We'll play it by ear, then,' or 'Once we touch base, we'll …' And he took even more pleasure saying them when speaking to a fellow Arab. He'd use the phrase and then say, like a hedonistic ritual, 'Mittel Bi-Oulou Bill Ingleeseh', 'As they say in English …'

Khadija, the Gambian housekeeper, now entered the dining room to place the last sumptuous dish prepared in the kitchen. On entering, her eyes lit up, espying Yusuf. She verily bloomed within the purple-black sheen of her dark skin as she came to kiss and greet her favourite. She stood back and looked Yusuf up and down, wagging a chunky index finger:

'You! You! You don't know cleanliness, you!'

And Yusuf replied, smiling deferentially, 'Yes, I know, I know: "Cleanliness is close to Godliness." You must pray for me, Haddy.' An eminently lightsome, bubbly spirit, she none the less took her Islam seriously, praying five times a day, fasting at the required seasons, and hoped to one day make the Hajj to Mecca. She was a gem out of Africa, with an elephantine heart quick to render her maudlin, and tearful. Before Yusuf would leave she'd serenade him and recite in a fluent whisper a verse from the Koran, which she'd learnt by rote; much as his maternal grandmother, now passed over, was wont to do. Mariam took pleasure in the ritual, for all her unbelief. Anything in the manner of cement and bonds between those she loved was a boon.

The evening, meanwhile, went smoothly, a baby's bum more savage. Said regaled his older brother with his news about applications to universities. Mahmoud ate till his shirt's buttons became so taut against his paunch that they threatened to burst free, fly off, with the petulance of hunted exiles. His mother was the reconnaissance and presiding spirit over the meal, the incumbent shadow to the various suns in and of her home.

***

As any woman might be, Lara was intrigued to learn of the whys and wherefores of this: her own chance, uncanny power. Like most women, she wanted a mirror to talk to her, to tell her of the large adventure of her allure. And this matchless curiosity led, over the next few weeks to the hale intrigue of their friendship: platonic, rather then erotic. And he made her laugh, which, again, is a banal, cheap, kitsch way of putting it; but then humour has its ways of disarming and subverting itself, a kind of somersault which makes anything go, which makes prodigal use of even its own flagrant failures; but that, only with the right kind of intelligence to gird and steer it.

It was, on the face of things, a match made in the garden of their young lives. Even the weeds were party to their simple passion and spoke the language of tulip, tulip and rose.

This evening, a few weeks into their courtship, Yusuf, bred to be a prince in the interstices and awkward spots of any situation, was feigning a momentary imbecility. It was a dumb show, a kind of obliging puppetry. The young woman opposite him had just made a flagrant Freudian slip and had subsequently burned plum.

So Yusuf was being 'noble.' It had grown into a habit since his university days. More than once his temperamental shyness, as translated into the ribaldry of late adolescence, came across as redolent with airs of superiority. They'd called him 'noble,' whether sincerely or sarcastically. Rarely was a young man of such a docile, peaceful temperament. But it bothered him at an almost visceral level, back at the time and ever since. The predicate insinuated he had a choice …

He now said, snapping out of his mute marionette, 'You were saying you wanted to be loved as by a dying painter.' It was said jaggedly, and out of the blue: not in any sense relevant to their prior conversation. Yusuf used it like an electric jolt, to sting and spur the two of them to talk in fire.

Lara had her hair trussed up in a bird-like bundle. It suggested either rushed, haphazard arrangement, or the artifice and sprezzatura of such. She wore vice-tight navy jeans and a tomato-red T-shirt. And this evening she was all ears (distinctly elfin ears): she'd not much to say for herself.

He waved the Moroccan waiter over, to order another round of drinks. He knew the fellow quite well. As a kind of happy digression he began to relate what he knew to Lara.

Ahmad had been in the country for over a decade. Spoke good English. He'd a pockmarked face, the colour of weeds under a propitious sun: a yellow at odds with his accommodating nature, and the practice of his trade. He was the son of a carpenter, who'd hawked his wares in the old markets of Marrakesh. Ahmad was the equivalent of a Formula One racer with the ins and outs of the hookah, as she could well see, by watching him negotiate the servicing of the place. He was prehensile, like a lizard.

Yusuf continued.

Before she married, Ahmad's mother was a poet of some ilk. Once they'd come to know each other from his frequent visits, Ahmad had told

Yusuf a little of his family history, and of the oaken tale of that sometime Marrakesh. There was a past — however much of a fluke in time and place — when his mother was in her early twenties, a burgeoning poet, when she was wont to walk into cafés and restaurants, announce herself as such, and was able subsequently to pay for her dinner and drinks with impromptu poems. Some were actually quite dexterous. For when she got home, she was in the habit of rewriting them from memory and storing them. In lilting Moroccan she'd called them 'the flowers of the happenstance.' Later, much later, Ahmad was still able to recite some. They'd a musicality that at times approached the virtuoso. Akin with this tense grip on the material thud or the material flue of words, was her early suicide, when she left Ahmad as a brave nine year old with his father. From the besotted love and the besotted memory of her, his father had never remarried — which was an exception, going by the mores of the time and place.

Yusuf had seen it all in sepia. And now, chin propped by an open palm, wide-eyed, Lara too was beguiled, though second-hand, by the lingering romance, the long-living traces after the small footsteps of a love. A sturdy love, then; unlike what, in the deepest cavern and lair of his heart, Yusuf had with Lara.

As he walked her to her home, which was, like his, in the environs of Kensington, a few stray, late-night partygoers littered the tree-lined streets. A few wild gawps, screeches, shouts. Under the artificial light of her apartment block's entrance, he kissed her. It was the second time they'd kissed, the first having been a complete blunder — if it wasn't for Yusuf's swift deployment of salving humour. This time, though, they were like tree to branch, like branch to leaf. And then, having turned to leave, he said to himself, somewhere between a thought and a whisper: '*Et in Arcadia Ego …*'

Just so, clichés sway into wells.

***

At that same Iranian bistro round the corner from his flat, Yusuf waited patiently for Nadim and his newly-engaged sister, Victoria. It was the third Sunday since Nadim had informed him about that incumbent engagement.

In one corner of the place Ahmad was weeping copious tears. Taking a five minute break from his duties, his mobile ringing persistently for the third time, he'd just been told by a somewhat distant uncle that his father had died. He was wailing and emitting pebble-shaped, pebble-sized tears, as though saltwater had become a language for sorrow. The owner sat at a distance, on the face of things looking upset at the disturbance to the humdrum running of his bistro, but deep down, like a true oriental, admiring and approving this ramshackle wake. It was just and in the order of things.

Later that evening, having progressed with his friends from mint-tea and grape-flavoured shishas, to bottled beer, to, finally, short vulva-shaped glasses of dry and iceless vodka, Yusuf, returned home and had a dream. Khadija was there. The tall and purple African was dancing to a bone-deep beat with those of her tribe round a fire — as though his dream-maker were in a fluster and mixing ethnic clichés. These preternaturally tall and fat West Africans were not lamenting; they were celebrating. All the dancers, as well as the chief who sat on a thatch throne, were driven by sheer merriment, exuded true joy from their pores, sweating into the night. They were rejoicing because a two-year-old boy had just died. When he was born, like all those born in that tribe, they had wailed and lamented, because yet another soul had to face the horrors of poverty, disease and dearth. Now, the boy having passed on, they were yelling in Wolof all sorts of melodic and unmelodic gratitude to their God. In the dream Khadija was wearing a skirt of thatch, like a denizen of the nineteenth century South Sea Islands. Something out of Conrad. And though they were giving thanks to the Muslim God and his Prophet, all the details and paraphernalia of the scenes in Yusuf's dream were as though composed by a very, very confused and ignorant craftsman. A painter with two eyes gouged out at birth, say. And funnily enough, still inside the dream, Yusuf had the sense that, even though he was an observer of the scenes, he was himself being watched, was himself another kind of 'scene' or tableau for a farther observer. Then these two layers began to meld and intermix. He woke up in giddy hysterics, without knowing what was so damned hilarious — only that that hilarity was of a depth, and so depth-charged, as to rattle his diaphragm like it was made of clunky metal, nearly making him choke on his dawning 'ha-ha-ha.'

***

When he woke up fully there was a woman shrieking outside. Her scream was of such a pin-like tenor that it actually reeked: if it can be said that a sound might have a smell.

After his shower, returning to his room while drying his hair, there was laughter from that same outdoors, shrill, shrill and warped, as though a cartoon had got obscenely drunk, and then acid-high, obscenely too, while watching a porno movie. But was that shrill laughter necessarily outside? Maybe it came from within his own baroque mind?

Maybe, just maybe, it was that peacock, his Icelandic neighbour? Maybe?

Yusuf now thought: 'This is getting too damned reflexive! I'm skating on thin ice.' So, he moved to the next section ...

2
Red Centurions

The place was frequented by Iranian ex-pats, Gulf Arabs, the odd stray Lebanese, Syrian or Egyptian (usually of the gay persuasion), Jews, Indians, cowboy-Russians — but only one Englishman. The owner hailed from some pre-revolutionary aristocratic family. He'd kept the idiosyncrasies of that antique, and for him, rose-tinted regime, however sullied by history's pointing fingers and dicta. As though Batista were some kind of saint, his corpulent body, his greedy bodying forth, rendered pristine, shriven, crystal. It was Mr Sohrab's 'pleasure' to allow one Englishman in his bistro at a time. And only one. He'd a taut view of the value of an Englishman — and this, in the fallen mêlée of Kensington, London. This type — his archetypal Englishman — was either the real thing, a kind of outdated milord, or was the type who allowed his women, his girls, to go drinking, wearing skirts with no panties.

To those in the know, a select few, Mr. Sohrab's Iranian bistro sold black market caviar from back home, or thereabouts. This morning the young lady who regularly supplied his bistro with the clandestine stuff had called in earlier, called in sick.

'That bloody pimp, that bloody bastard! I'll kill him,' Mr. Sohrab had said.

'No really, it's nothing. You can't blame him — he didn't know what he was doing, that he was carrying the illness ...'

'Not know! What do you mean, not know? He gave you syphilis and gonorrhoea and genital crabs! Why, I'll chop off his balls; just say the word! Or just one ball, huh? So the other stays as witness and shame ...'

One of the waiters in his place had made Lina a paramour. They'd a physical chemistry from the first time she'd driven in to deliver the illicit stock of caviar. Within a month they were having sex like sex-famished rabbits. Ahmad, the other waiter, had warned her off him, knowing his colleague for the dog that he was. But even he didn't know the extent to which the libido of his colleague, Rumi, had splayed and laid itself across and within hookers most evenings — a traveller in more than one orifice — rendering him bearer of all sorts of unwashed unease.

Later that day, when Rumi arrived for his shift, Mr. Sohrab, indignant, berated him in front of coevals and clients alike.

'Why you, you, you ...' He huffed, holding up a fist at Rumi's chin. 'What made you think you could get away with such a caper? Who do you think you are: Valentino?'

'But it wasn't me. She must've got all those diseases from someone else.' On the verge of tears, Rumi dithered, pretty but not quite mensch.

'Lina is like a daughter to me you blackguard, you crook! Her father saved many lives, including mine in the Eighties. And now you, you knave, you dirty knave ... I am going to cut one of your balls off, OK? I promised her ...'

'My balls?'

'Ah, now you don't look so sexy, huh? What would it be like, you, you pseudo-Casanova, you bastard: how would you like to seduce women, young innocent women, gems, with only a single ball? I'd like to see you go at it like that, huh!'

Ahmad was laughing compulsively a little to the side.

Mr. Sohrab turned to him with venom in his eyes.

'Oh, so you too, you too want to walk around with one ball, huh? How will it look, the two of you, both with a single ball in a nut-sack made for two …' A smile slowly stole across his face: he'd just amused himself. 'And then the two of you can go out together, fuck each other, one ball to one ball — Hah!' He bellowed with laughter, much pleased with the prospect.

'Yeah, two one-balled warriors!'

***

Yusuf was in a quandary. He'd been seeing Lara for just under two months; he knew it was going nowhere.

Presently, he was sitting at the Iranian, as ever, on one of the outriding tables, nestled beside the caged thigh-like billowing flames used to warm the space — toking gently on a ponderous cigarette. When Lara arrived they kissed in greeting. She was dressed in a navy suit, blazer and skirt, with a pristine white shirt. Regular vestments for lawyers working near Holborn.

About twenty minutes in, Lara, having belaboured her current litany of sorrows — such as her schizophrenic dad and her junky brother and the infinite boredom of her work as a corporate lawyer — Yusuf said, curtly, 'I think we shouldn't see each other anymore. I mean: not this way.'

A staggered silence of twenty seconds, feeling like minutes, ensued. Twice Lara was on the verge of saying something, and twice she stopped herself.

'You mean,' she now said, looking troubled, 'you mean, you've met someone else?'

'No, it's just I don't think I'm in the right place, personally, to take things to the next level, which, I presume, would be serious.'

'Someone what: prettier than me, funnier than me, what …?'

At this point Ahmad asked them for their order. Yusuf waved him off. But he persisted, asked Lara again, specifically.

'Ahmad, my friend, we're having a serious conversation. Please go. We'll order, if we're going to order, in ten minutes … Please …'

'I'll have a glass of vodka on the rocks, a double,' Lara interjected.

Ahmad smiled, graciously, and hurried off.

'So now you're going to hit the booze?'

'I can do as I please. We, 'us', well, it's no longer a thing. I don't see what claim you have on me, my drinking habits …'

A minute's silence ensued: they faced each other like two disarmed gladiators, like two clowns without a smile between them.

'Look, is there anything you want to know: I mean, we'll still be friends, but is there any question or questions you want answered?'

For a split-second a look of shock stole across Lara's face.

When the vodka arrived she guzzled it in two quick instalments, Yusuf looked on with sadness or annoyance, or somewhere mingling in between.

Mr. Sohrab came over, and said, 'Welcome, welcome, young sir. So glad to have you and your lovely girlfriend at my joint once again. Most welcome.' With one arm on each of them, as if to include their evident relationship within the import of his own desires and the place itself, which bodied forth those very ideals, he said, 'And do I hear wedding bells? You should you know. You make such a lovely couple …'

85

Yusuf tried to smile over his gritted teeth. Lara burst into tears and then covered her face with both hands. Mr. Sohrab's face was the epitome of mystification. Lara stood up, then Yusuf stood up, then Lara let out a brief yelp and ran off.

'What is wrong?' Mr Sohrab asked. Yusuf told him.

'But why? You do, you do make a great couple. And I've seen you here together many times and I always said to myself: "Now there is a wholesome couple. What the earth was made for. Like two swans on a lake; like two penguins being funny together in the snow; like …"' While he searched for a third simile, Yusuf put down a five pound note, gathered his bag, and, tapping Mr. Sohrab, who was still mid-daydream, said quickly,

'I have to go.'

Mr Sohrab was about to protest, when he was called to the phone. He sighed wistfully, looked up at God as though at a fellow-traveller in disappointment, and went in to take the call. It was Lina, daughter of his old comrade, calling to say she couldn't deliver the caviar that afternoon, because she was ill. After persistent, avuncular questioning, Mr. Sohrab rang off and looked in the direction of Rumi, his eyes like red centurions.

***

It was two-thirty in the morning. Yusuf and Nadim were sitting at the Iranian, at which they'd stopped on the way back from Victoria, Nadim's sister's, wedding bash. The place was unique in West Kensington for having a license 'till four in the morning.

Both young men were evidently drunk and both slurring their words. But both being so, they managed to understand each other.

'So, no more shenanigans.'

'No more shenanigans, in truth.'

'The old girl's hitched, tessellated — that is a word? — collared, muzzled ... what have you ...'

'Your sister's now settled, married, yes, I agree.'

'Clearly.'

'And I, I am alone in love again. There,' he now said, pointing at the owner of the place, Mr Sohrab, 'that chap was ministering angel at our split. Poor chap: I think he liked the idea of us as a couple frequenting his place.'

'And why is it, Yiz, you can never keep up a longish relationship? You're nearly thirty, no?'

'I fear the Ides of March.'

'What?'

'Nothing: just felt like saying that.'

'You're drunk, old buddy, old pal.'

'We both are.'

Ahmad, the Moroccan waiter, now idled over and asked them their order.

'I will have a Big Mac and fries.'

Ahmad, grinning, now turned to Nadim and said, seamlessly, as it were:

'And you, sir: perhaps some chicken nuggets, a milkshake? A caramel sundae?' He chucked his head back and chuckled.

Motioning with his arms as though to clear the debris, the metaphorical debris in front of them, Yusuf said, 'We will have lamb and saffron rice. And we will have two glasses of the Rioja.'

Ahmad said, 'The Rioja is not available by the glass, only by the bottle.'

Nadim bellowed: 'And so, the bottle it is. In honour of my sister, a now-kept woman.'

Half-way through their meal, they noticed a ruckus at the front of the Iranian. It seemed like there were some true-blood English trying to occupy a table. But Mr. Sohrab was as ever adamant that there be a maximum of one Englishman, true blood, in his place at a time. There already was one, bevelled somewhere indoors near the grill. Thus, no room for more. He tried to explain this to the group of Englishmen.

'As you can see, my sirs, this is an Iranian restaurant populated by all the nations, all the genders, all the sexes and all the orientations, except the Englishman. I permit only one at a time. There is one here presently. In conclusion ...'

'But this restaurant is in Kensington. Kensington is in London. London is the capital of England ...'

'Precisely,' Mr. Sohrab said, as if his argument was uncannily clinched.

'What do you mean by precisely?'

'Well,' Mr. Sohrab continued, 'it's a question of aesthetics.'

'What do you mean: aesthetics?'

'The pale white skin of the Englishman has no place in this painting, except as an aleatory detail, which happenstance puts into relief the non-English nature of my island in this grubby England.'

The three young Englishman were baffled.

'If you gentlemen would wait, say, half-an-hour, then the current Englishman will have left. I will then allow one of you at a time a seat, say, twenty minutes each ...'

'Excuse me?'

'OK, so: then half-an-hour each ...'

'But this is a restaurant, not a bloody painting!'

'No, young sirs, it is a painting. A painting, nothing but a painting.'

'Well, then, fuck your bloody Rembrandt!' And they stomped off.

Mr. Sohrab grinned with glee inwardly:

because, of course, Rembrandt was an Iranian ...

Despite his sadness, indeed as an uncanny part of it, Yusuf couldn't help but chuckle. Here was Dickens, here was Waugh, here was Naipaul. And all of it lost to the world. He continued to ponder, though it was no doubt academic now, what kind of subtext lay hidden in both the fact that Yusuf was the last person he'd contacted, if by email, and that Karim had done it by attaching some writing — some writing ostensibly dedicated to him.

Indeed: *What was it about humour?* Time and time again he'd noticed how quick wits were cognate with a certain kind of chronic melancholia: a continuing barter with death. For humour meant Imagination, a ranging elsewhere in the here-and-now. So that Imagination meant the constant presence of absence, the Other (with death as ultimate instance of the latter). Humour, Yusuf now thought, is thus a type of anxiety: but the anxiety of the Omnipotent. Lecturing to himself, he developed the idea:

The anxiety of God is indicative, like all anxiety, of some lack (which gap, again, is revealing of death's own bower). Except, with this character-type, the lack was at a second order: it was the lack of the lack of lack. Comedy, it now occurred to Yusuf, was Christian, or Trinitarian, in its very essence. God (Who's no lack) invents and deploys against Himself the requisite lack, by killing Himself. And that's how He lives (for and in and by our imaginations): He lives and is alive and redolent for us because He did the only damage He was susceptible to: self-damage. Christ was the apogee of exile, Yusuf concluded, and He was a comedian.

Wednesday

Though it was declared a university holiday, Wednesday was over for Yusuf before it started.

He'd got drunk the night before, by himself. He'd slept in, as a matter of course, and didn't get out of bed 'till one o'clock that afternoon. Getting out of bed, he'd rushed immediately to the bathroom and vomited for a good five minutes.

His dream lingered, woven from the stuff of sheer cliff-edge and vile horror. In it, he'd been asked to give the eulogy at Karim's funeral. He'd given the following speech, pocked by the odd monstrous intrusion …

Perhaps the man who has everything is the true lost sheep.

This young man, brilliant and handsome and caring and funny was more the wiseacre than the rest of us, our years summed and totted and in the balance, put together.

Who knows what horrors went through his mind the night he ended his own life?

But rest assured: his wasn't a denial of life. Like a cancer, his death was from an abundance of life.

The man who takes his life still puts a premium on his suffering and the vale that is living in this world we've made for ourselves, as though out of ash and motes …

At this point, Robbie, strangely attending the funeral,

had quoted Dietrich Bonhoeffer in a very loud voice, interjecting between Yusuf's sentences:

"A man's own decision here becomes the cause of his death," yet, "one may still distinguish between direct self-destruction and this surrendering of life into the hand of God."

Robbie then vanished into thin air. Yusuf started up once again. When he looked up, though, from the printed sheet bearing his speech, the church was empty. Not a single soul left. Irrespective, he continued to the echoic emptiness ...

We are all dying. But death, death is a death to death.

Our mortality is the only thing, ultimately, that bars us from the home of happiness.

So ...

At this point, the church still empty, Yusuf thought he espied Latifa and Cynthia making-out voluptuously in a far corner, under a sort of, no, a distinctly Gothic arch. He continued, though, unruffled.

No, the true suicide, the man who truly wishes to negate life: he is the man who lives, the man who lives on ...

Biography

Omar Sabbagh is a widely published poet and critic. His poetry collections include *My Only Ever Oedipal Complaint* (2010) and *The Square Root of Beirut* (2012 — both from Cinnamon Press); a fourth collection, *To The Middle Of Love*, will be published by Cinnamon Press in late 2016.

In 2014, he took up an Assistant Professorship in English at the American University in Dubai.

Lightning Source UK Ltd.
Milton Keynes UK
UKHW022011061020
371120UK00008B/514